PERSIAN FOLKTALES

In the same series

BRETON FOLKTALES

RUSSIAN FOLKTALES

CHINESE FOLKTALES

Persian Folktales

LONDON: G. BELL & SONS 1971

PUBLISHED BY G. BELL & SONS LTD,
YORK HOUSE, 6 PORTUGAL STREET, LONDON, WC2

PRINTED IN GREAT BRITAIN BY
NORTHUMBERLAND PRESS LTD, GATESHEAD

ISBN 0 7135 1727 1

ORIGINALLY PUBLISHED AS *Persische Volksmärchen*
TRANSLATED INTO GERMAN BY ARTHUR CHRISTENSEN, 1958
THIS SELECTION TRANSLATED FROM THE GERMAN BY
ALFRED KURTI

CONTENTS

1. THE STORY OF ALI MUHAMMAD'S MOTHER

MANY years ago there lived in the town of Shiraz a man and a woman who had five or six children. Their eldest son was called Ali Muhammad, and for that reason the man and the woman grew accustomed to calling themselves Ali Muhammad's father and Ali Muhammad's mother. Unfortunately, Ali Muhammad's mother made life very difficult for her husband by her incessant chatter; however, for the sake of his children he felt he could not very well get rid of her. Finally, the man could no longer stand the constant babble; he only wished that she would die and he thought to himself: 'I think I had better take her along to the Tcha Quala Bandar[1] and push her over the side so that I shall at long last be rid of this misery.'

So he said one day to his wife: 'Have you ever visited the Tcha Qala Bandar?'—'No,' she replied. 'In that case you had better come along with me, because it is well worth visiting.' They left the children at home and climbed up to the gorge. 'Bend down,' said her husband, 'and see how deep it is there.' Just as she bent over to look down into the depths her husband pushed her from behind and she fell into the gorge. He then went home, thinking that from now on he would be able to live in peace.

When he returned to his house, however, all his children, Ali Muhammad, Hassan, Husein, Sakine and Gul Banu,[2] crowded around him, asking: 'Where is our mother?' And they all started weeping. Their father spoke kindly to them and tried his best to calm them but it was of no avail—they cried and wailed. Thus three days went by and the children's lament grew louder from one hour to the next. Ali Muhammad's father felt so miserable that he was reminded of Ali Muhammad's mother a thousand times a day. He only wished that he had broken his own neck rather than do such a stupid deed; it would certainly have been better for the children. On the fourth day, when he realized that things were going from bad to worse and the children were crying and wailing more than ever, he said to himself: 'It seems I have no choice but to take a rope and climb up to the gorge again. I shall then tell her that I will pull her out on condition that she promises to stop her constant bickering and nagging.'

And so he took a rope and went to the Tcha Qala Bandar. When he reached the gorge he bent over the edge and called: 'Ali Muhammad's mother, Ali Muhammad's mother!'—'Yes,' a voice answered from the bottom. He continued: 'If you promise not to nag and scold and chatter, I will lower the rope to you and haul you up again.'—'Yes,' the voice replied, 'I am truly sorry about my past behaviour.' The man let the rope down into the cave and said: 'Hold on tightly, I am going to pull now!'—'I am holding tight,' the voice said. Ali Muhammad's father pulled on the rope. It was terribly heavy, as if it carried twice or three times his wife's weight. 'This is very strange,' he thought. 'One would have imagined that she had lost weight for lack of food but now, on the contrary, she is three times as heavy.' Just the same he kept pulling with all his strength, and when he had finally hoisted the end of the rope as far as the entrance to the gorge, he was curious to see whether his wife had indeed put on so much weight; then he saw that a huge serpent had wound itself around the rope and had come up with it.

The man was so frightened he nearly let go of the rope again, dropping the serpent back into the gorge, but the serpent begged him: 'For God's sake, rescue me from Ali Muhammad's mother! For the past three days and nights she chattered and nagged and scolded so much that she nearly drove me out of my mind. If you are willing to help me now I shall reward you with a deed for which you will always be grateful to me.'—'What do you propose doing for me?' the man asked. 'Frankly, I am more concerned about her children than about her.' The serpent said: 'I shall crawl along and coil myself round the neck of the king's daughter and it will be absolutely impossible for anyone to remove me from there until you appear.'—'All right,' said the man; he released the serpent, left the woman down in the gorge and went away.

As promised, the serpent made its way to the king's daughter and coiled itself round her neck. The following day the whole town resounded with cries of lament. The king's servants were sent out to fetch all Rammals,[3] makers of talismans and soothsayers to the palace so that they might with their prayers and magic chase away the serpent—but it was all in vain. The king then swore a solemn oath, promising that he who succeeded in removing the serpent from his daughter's neck should have her as his wife. Thereafter, large crowds, disguised as Rammals and soothsayers, flocked to the palace but none of them had any luck and the princess was nearly dying. Finally, Ali Muhammad's father placed a turban on his head and sat down at a street corner with a Raml[3] in front of him. One of the king's servants, who was searching the town for soothsayers, happened to pass and asked him: 'Do you know anything of the art of driving away a serpent from the king's daughter?'—'Yes,' he replied. 'Arise, because if this is indeed so, your fortune will be assured.' They went to the sultan. The unfortunate ruler, who had had neither peace nor rest since the day the great calamity befell his daughter, turned to Ali Muhammad's father and said: 'If you succeed in ridding my daughter of the serpent, you shall be my son-in-law and share with me the king's power.'—'Your majesty need have no fear,' replied Ali Muhammad's father.

They led Ali Muhammad's father to the chambers of the princess. He said: 'Leave us alone because my magic cannot work in the presence of others.' They all went out and Ali Muhammad's father went up to the serpent, whispering: 'A promise must always be kept.'—'So be it,' the serpent replied, 'but I warn you that if I ever wind myself round the neck of another woman, you must not interfere, or I shall kill you.' He accepted this condition, and the serpent uncoiled itself and slid away. There was great rejoicing everywhere at the release of the princess. The sultan gave orders for the town to be decorated for seven days and nights of festivities; the wedding of the princess and Ali Muhhamad's father was celebrated and they lived in happiness and joy.

As far as the serpent was concerned, it went straight from Shiraz to the kingdom of China and coiled itself round the neck of the daughter of the king of China. The people of China also tried in vain to drive away the pernicious creature. Finally, a man arrived who told the king that the son-in-law of the king of Iran knew of a magic spell by which he was able to chase away the serpent simply by blowing on it, because some time ago the serpent had coiled itself also round the neck of the daughter of the king of Iran and this man, who was now that king's son-in-law, had driven it away. The king of China therefore despatched his Grand Vizier to the land of Iran with magnificent gifts to ask the king of Iran to allow his son-in-law to travel to China so that, by his noble character and love for his fellow human beings, he might be so kind as to rid the princess of the serpent. The Chinese Grand Vizier duly arrived in the land of Iran and delivered his message to the king. The latter proved willing and commanded his son-in-law to travel to China forthwith. Ali Muhammad's father now found himself in a terrible dilemma because the serpent had, after all, threatened to kill him, and yet he could not very well avoid making the journey. And so he set off for China. On the way he thought about the problem and finally an idea occurred to him as to how to drive the serpent away.

At long last he arrived in China. The king of China rode out in person from his palace to receive the traveller with all the honours due to a son-in-law of the king of Iran, and conducted him to the royal palace. After a few days, Ali Muhammad's father asked for permission to enter the suite of the princess. On entering, he said in a loud and clear voice: 'You people of China, how can you sit here so calmly? Are you not aware that Ali Muhammad's mother has escaped from the Tcha Qala Bandar and is on her way to China? She will arrive here and enter this chamber any minute!'

No sooner had the serpent heard the name of Ali Muhammad's mother than it released its hold on the neck of the princess, and no one knows where it fled to.

2. THE BIRD CALLED FLOWER TRILL

THERE once lived a king who had three sons: the first was called Malik Muhammad, the second Malik Djamsheed and the third Malik Ibrahim. The king loved his youngest son, Malik Ibrahim, best of all and this caused enmity on the part of the other two brothers. One day, the king fell ill and not a single physician in the whole country knew of a cure for his disease. Finally, one of them said: 'We know of just one remedy—if only it could be found.' 'What is it?' asked the people. The physician replied: 'There is a green fish in the sea and on its tail it carries a golden ring. If that fish is caught and cut up and the pieces are placed on the Sultan's heart, he is sure to recover.'

The king's sons went down to the beach and offered large sums of gold to the divers. After searching along the sea shore for several days, the divers succeeded in catching the fish and brought it to Malik Ibrahim. The prince took the fish and was surprised at its beauty. Suddenly he noticed an inscription on its forehead and, looking more closely, he read these words: 'There is no God but Allah, Muhammad is his prophet and Ali his representative.' On seeing these words, Malik Ibrahim was deeply moved and said: 'Even though my father's health would be restored by this fish, I could never kill it.' And he threw the fish back into the sea. When his brothers and the viziers, who were expecting to be given the fish, saw Malik Ibrahim's action, they bit their fingers with surprise, not knowing at first what to say to the king. But then

Malik Muhammad and Malik Djamsheed, who had been waiting for just such an opportunity, ran straight to their father and told him what had happened. The king grew angry and said: 'If Malik Ibrahim is waiting for me to die so that he may become king, I will this very instant deprive him of all his rights as a son and heir.'

The king's illness became so much worse, however, that he did not have a moment's peace. The same physician's advice was sought again. He said: 'There remains only one more remedy. There is a bird called Flower Trill. Each time he sings he drops a flower from his beak. If anyone is fortunate enough to catch this bird, and if one of the flowers that have dropped from its beak is placed upon the king's heart, his illness will be cured.' The king kissed both his sons on their foreheads and said: 'You are my only hope. Go forth at once to find the bird called Flower Trill.'

The princes prepared themselves for the journey that very hour, and set off to search all over the world for the bird called Flower Trill. When Malik Ibrahim learned that his two brothers had gone away to find the bird called Flower Trill, he took a few pieces of gold and also rode out of the town. On the way he met his brothers. 'Where are you going?' they asked him. 'I am searching for the same bird as you.'—'All right,' they said, 'in that case let us ride together.'

To cut a long story short, the king's sons rode for many days and nights until they reached a crossroads where there was a tree and a spring. The three sons dismounted to rest for a while. After the other two had fallen asleep, Malik Ibrahim arose and went for a walk. Suddenly he came across a stone tablet which bore this inscription: 'Those who pass this crossroads should know that the path leading off to the right is safe and easy, but the path to the left is so dangerous that the traveller has no hope of ever returning. Should anyone wish to travel along the left-hand road in spite of this, however, he must take this tablet with him.' Malik Ibrahim memorized the writing on the tablet, went back to his brothers and found that they were still asleep. He woke them and said: 'Read what is written on this tablet and choose the road you wish to follow.' After reading the inscription, the two princes said: 'We will continue along the right-hand road because our father is waiting impatiently for us to return with the bird called Flower Trill.' Malik Ibrahim, however, said: 'I shall take the road to the left.' His brothers urged him to continue his journey with them along the right-hand road, but to no avail. So they bade each other farewell, the two brothers taking the road to the right and Malik Ibrahim turning to the left. Let us leave the two brothers to their fate and see how Malik Ibrahim fared.

After a few days and nights he reached the gate of a beautiful and refreshing garden. He entered and saw that the garden was rich with fruit trees and that little brooks rippled and flowed in all directions. The prince tethered his horse to a tree, stretched out his hand and plucked a few apples. He ate some of them and put the others into his saddle bag, for he was prudent enough to realize that his travels may take him to places where no food was to be found. Then he strolled in the garden for a little while. He came to a tall building, but try as he might he was unable to discover any other human beings. He stopped in surprise, thinking to himself: 'Who could be the owner of such a garden in the middle of the desert?' Suddenly the sound of splashing water reached his ears.

He turned round and saw a young girl, radiant as the sun, sitting at the edge of a pool and playing with the water.

When he saw this beautiful girl, Malik Ibrahim lost his heart to her. At the same moment she noticed him. She rose and, approaching him, said in a friendly, soft voice: 'Oh Malik Ibrahim, oh sweet prince, how did you find your way here? For years I have longed for your arrival.' Astonished beyond belief, Malik Ibrahim asked himself: 'What is this, how does this girl know my name? This is truly a riddle.' But he had fallen so deeply in love that he no longer cared for anything else. And so, taking each other by the hand, they entered the castle and the girl did all she could to captivate the prince's heart.

Meanwhile, a thought had occurred to the prince. He rose to go out. The girl tried to detain him but he reassured her with an eloquent speech and went out of the castle. In a corner of the garden he pulled out the stone tablet and read the words written on it: 'You, who have chosen the road to the left, will find a beautiful garden and a seductive girl. Act wisely and do not be captivated by her lovely face because she is really a cunning old sorceress who wants to kill you. At first you must be kind to her and if she proposes that you wrestle with her, accept her suggestion, but while wrestling you must pull down her gown. On the left side of her body she has a black mole and this is where you must drive in your dagger with all your might. Take care not to miss, or you will be turned into a black stone for all eternity.'

The prince replaced the tablet and returned to the castle where the girl was waiting for him impatiently. When she saw him she started caressing him once again. After a few words of love, the girl said: 'Come, let us wrestle with each other to see which of us is the stronger.' He agreed and they started to wrestle. The prince suddenly became aware that she was about to cast a spell to change him into something else. Praying for God's help, he pulled down the girl's gown. She tried to fend him off but he thrust his dagger handle-deep into the black mole. At once a terrible tornado arose, accompanied by thunder and lightning, and Malik Ibrahim fainted with fear. When he regained consciousness, he saw the corpse of an old, withered woman lying beside him on the ground. There was no trace of the garden, nor of the castle; all that could be seen was the parched, arid desert stretching out around him in all directions. He said a prayer of thanks, mounted his horse and continued his journey.

After a few days and nights he reached a garden similar to the first one. He entered and in the centre of the garden he saw a large lake. Out on the lake a small vessel was moving. The prince tethered his horse to a tree, untied the saddle bag and took it with him to the shore of the lake. He then swam over to the vessel and climbed on board. There he found ten men lying sprawled on the deck, all as dead as stone, with the exception of one in whom there was still a tiny spark of life. Malik Ibrahim tried to question him but the man was unable to speak.

He then took a few apples from his saddle bag, cut them into small pieces and fed the survivor. The old man, who was nearly dying from starvation, soon felt his strength returning and sat up, and the prince started questioning him: 'Where do you come from and who are these dead people?' The man replied: 'We are from Gulabetun.[1] We heard that there is a city opposite the Qaf mountains,[2] that the mountains themselves consist of pure gold, and that at the foot of those mountains there flows a river of silver. I and a few other wealthy merchants made preparations for a journey of discovery to that city, but we had no idea of its whereabouts. For nearly ten years we have travelled from one city to another, from one country to the next, without ever finding a clue to our gold. Ten days ago we happened to arrive at the gate of this garden. On entering we noticed this vessel, and for our amusement we went on board the ship, which was then lying by the shore of the lake. The ship moved away at once and took us to the centre of the lake. Throughout the past ten days the ship has circled around without moving forwards or backwards, as though it were caught in a whirlpool. Each day at noon a hand appears from the water and drags one us down into the depths, no matter whether he be dead or alive. At first there were twenty of us; ten have already been seized by the hand and the others have starved to death. There is only one hour left now before the hand is due to appear again.'

Malik Ibrahim pulled out his tablet and read: 'After you have killed the first witch and have reached the other garden with the lake and the vessel, take care not to be seduced by the sweet and tempting words that the owner of the hand will say to you, because she is the sister of the first witch. You must squeeze the hand with all your might so that the spell may be broken. Should you be vanquished in the struggle, you will lose your freedom for ever.' The prince replaced the tablet and waited. Suddenly he saw a hand rising from the water, more beautiful and delicate than any hand he had ever seen before, and at the same time he heard a voice saying to him: 'Welcome, Malik Ibrahim, you who have had to overcome such difficulties to reach this place. Come now and let us shake hands in friendship.'—'With the greatest pleasure,' replied the prince, and the two hands gripped each other tightly and each started pulling in its own direction. The prince noticed that his opponent kept dragging him further and further down into the waves, and he was nearly defeated; then he commended his soul to God and squeezed his adversary's hand with such strength that he crushed it. A terrible storm broke out, just as on the previous occasion, accompanied by thunder and lightning, and a short while later the two men saw the body of an old witch lying in the midst of the immense desert in which they now found themselves. Malik Ibrahim asked the old man where he was thinking of going next and he replied: 'Wherever you may go, I want to follow as your servant.' But Malik Ibrahim answered: 'You are not strong enough to follow me where I intend to go. Therefore, go forth wherever you wish and may the Lord's peace be with you.' And so they parted.

Malik Ibrahim travelled on until he reached a place where there was a very tall tree and a spring. A large crowd of apes had gathered underneath the tree and one of them wore on its back a cloth made of cashmere wool, which was probably meant to signify that it was superior to the others. Behind the tree there was a well. The prince immediately pulled his stone tablet from amongst the folds of his robe and read what was written there: 'You, who have now slain the second witch, will come to a tree, and a well wherein the third witch dwells. You must descend into the well, and after passing a narrow corridor will reach a wide open plain where a tall building has been erected. Enter the building and there you will meet a girl, who is the witch in question. She will tempt you with cunning and trickery, but you must throw this stone tablet at her forehead and so split her head; this will break the magic spell.'

After reading this, Malik Ibrahim descended into the well and, as instructed by the words on the tablet, he killed the third witch.

As soon as he emerged from the well, he saw that all the apes had assumed human form and had become young maidens, each as beautiful as a full moon in the heavens; but there was one among them whose beauty put both the sun and the moon to shame. She wore a cloth of cashmere wool. The prince approached her and asked from which country she and the other girls had come, and in what manner they had fallen into the witch's hands. The girl replied: 'I am the daughter of the King of the Peris and my name is Maimune Khatun. One day, when walking outside the city with some of my slaves, I saw a gazelle with a beautiful spotted coat. I hurried after it, followed by my slaves, and we chased the gazelle for many miles until we finally reached a forest. Suddenly we saw the gazelle turn round and transform itself into an old, ugly woman and in a few seconds she had turned us into the shape in which you found us. When my father learned what had happened he sent out his army many times to fight the old witch, but she defeated them all with her sorcery. Praised be the Lord, for you have at long last released us. We shall be indebted to you until the Last Day and you may be sure that my father will reward you when he hears of our deliverance.'—'Maimune Khatun,' said Malik Ibrahim, 'if it pleases the Lord, I shall restore you safely to your father.'

They all continued their journey and reached the city of the Peris. Maimune went to her father and when he saw his child, whom he loved as his own soul, he hugged her and asked how she had managed to escape the witch's power. Maimune Khatun told her father how it had all come about. Thereupon the King of the Peris summoned Malik Ibrahim, kissed him on both cheeks and said: 'My dear young man, I once made a promise that he who succeeded in freeing Maimune should receive my kingdom and my daughter, for she is my only child. Though I did have a son, he departed this mortal world after Maimune had fallen into the witch's clutches, but the worst part of this tragedy is that every morning my son's body, wrapped in torn shrouds, is found to have been thrown out of his grave. He is reburied every day, but the following day this is all repeated. I have placed guards at his grave but none of them have so far been able to discover what is happening.'

Malik Ibrahim thought to himself: 'Surely the same witchcraft is at work here.' He then returned to the King of the Peris and said: 'It would be best if, before celebrating our wedding, we first settled the matter of your son. Whatever the connection may be between these strange things, there must be witchcraft involved, and I shall not rest until I have cleared up this mystery.'

The King of the Peris gave orders for Malik Ibrahim to be conducted to the grave of the Peri prince. Upon arrival, he dismissed the servants; he did not need them there. Then he hid alone behind a big stone and looked at his tablet. It said: 'You, who have now slain the third witch, will come to the city of the Peris where two witches have put a spell upon the son of the Peri king. To release the prince, you must sever both their heads at the same time with a single blow.' The prince hid the tablet next to his chest and waited. After the first half of the night had passed, he saw two wizened old women who were murmuring magic words. One of them carried a stick in her hand and the other had a thin twig under her arm. They approached the grave and started working their magic by blowing with their mouths, thereby turning themselves into two fourteen-year-old girls. Then one of them held her stick over the grave, and at once the prince's dead body fell out of his coffin. The girl murmured some more magic words and blew on him, whereupon he rose into a sitting position. 'Obey our commands,' they said, 'or we will break these sticks over your body.' The Peri prince turned away, refusing to submit to their will, and the terrible women raised their sticks, ready to let them crash down on the prince's body, but at that very moment Malik Ibrahim cut off both their heads in one single blow. A terrible storm arose, the wind howled and fearsome voices could be heard; but after a while the air became calm again, and the Peri prince threw himself at Malik Ibrahim's feet, calling out: 'You who have freed me, I will be your obedient slave as long as I live.' Then they both went hand in hand to the royal palace.

When the king received the news that Malik Ibrahim and the Peri prince were on their way he hurried out, barefoot and with uncovered head, to receive them. First he threw himself into the dust before Malik Ibrahim and said: 'We will all be your obedient servants and the kingdom shall be yours!' He then embraced his son and finally he turned to the vizier, saying: 'Prepare everything for the wedding of Maimune and Malik Ibrahim, and give orders that the whole city be decorated for the festivities.' As a sign of obedience the vizier placed a finger over his eye.

And so it came to pass that the city revelled in festive joy for seven days and seven nights. After the wedding had been celebrated, however, Malik Ibrahim approached the King of the Peris, asking for leave to continue his journey. 'Do you wish to leave us so soon?' the king asked him, and he replied: 'I must travel on because my father is waiting impatiently for the bird called Flower Trill and, wherever it may be found, I will catch it and bring it to my father.' Upon hearing the words 'A bird called Flower Trill', the King of the Peris thought for a short while. He then ordered all the Peris to assemble at the palace and when they had all arrived, he asked: 'Is there anyone among you who knows the whereabouts of the bird called Flower Trill?' One of them stepped forward from the crowd and said: 'I know where he lives. Nobody dares to enter his territory for fear of the Divs, however, because this bird belongs to a daughter of the King of the Peris on the Mountain of Qaf, and thousands of mighty Divs keep guard on him. The only thing I can do is to take Malik Ibrahim to the place where the Divs are keeping watch.' The King of the Peris turned to Malik Ibrahim and asked: 'What shall I do now?' The prince replied: 'Order them to take me to that place, and leave the rest to me.'

So the king gave orders for Malik Ibrahim to be escorted to the land of the Divs. One of the Peris assumed the form of a bird, took Malik Ibrahim on his back and soared into the air. After a flight of several hours he set the prince down on the ground and said: 'I dare not go any farther but I will wait here for three days to take you back to Maimune Khatun, but if you are not here within that time I will have to assume that you have been eaten by the Divs.'

Malik Ibrahim commended his soul to the Lord and walked on, right up to the Divs. When the Divs noticed the scent of a human in the air, they looked in every direction and finally saw Malik Ibrahim. Then they fell upon him. Malik Ibrahim, however, had not the slightest intention of becoming involved in a fight with them because he knew only too well that this would be like being caught between hammer and anvil. Instead, he uttered numerous apologies and said: 'A very urgent reason has brought me here.' When the Divs saw that he was a pleasant and eloquent young man, they took pity on him and asked what that urgent reason was. He replied: 'For a whole year I have crossed deserts and climbed mountains, and I have killed five witches; I came into the land of the Peris and made contact with them, but I have not come across that which I set forth to find and now I have been directed to this place so that I may find it.'—'And for what are you searching?' asked the Divs. 'It is the bird called Flower Trill,' he replied. The Divs looked at each other and said: 'Yes, it is quite true that the bird called Flower Trill is in that fortress over there on the right which belongs to Tarfe Banu, the daughter of the Peri King on the Mountain of Qaf. We are all here to guard the bird, so how can we steal it for you? Besides, we are not allowed to enter the fortress at all. If you succeed somehow in acquiring the bird yourself, however, we shall gladly take you from here to any place you wish.' The prince said: 'This is quite sufficient, I do not ask for anything else.'

So one of the Divs took him as far as the gate of Tarfe Banu's garden. It was broad daylight but everyone within the fortress lay fast asleep. Malik Ibrahim crept in very softly and, guided by the chirping voice of the bird called Flower Trill, he found his way to a large room where Tarfe Banu was sleeping. There he saw a girl of indescribable beauty lying on a bed decorated with precious stones which shone in all colours. In a golden cage hanging near her head perched the bird called Flower Trill and each time he trilled, sweet-scented and beautifully-coloured flowers fell from his beak. Malik Ibrahim calmly stretched out his hand, took the cage and returned to the Divs the way he had come. They asked him: 'Where do you want us to take you?' and he replied: 'Take me to the vicinity of my own country.' One of the Divs took him on his shoulders and, blowing through his nostrils like a smoking chimney, rose skywards. When they reached the cross-roads where Malik Ibrahim had found the stone tablet, he ordered the Div to descend. The Div set him down and gave him a few of his hairs, which in case of need he could burn to summon the Div, and the Div then returned to his homeland.[3]

Malik Ibrahim hung the cage containing the bird on a tree, sat down for a little rest and fell asleep. It so happened that his brothers, who were returning empty-handed from their search along the road leading off to the right, came past just at that moment. When they saw the sleeping Malik Ibrahim and the bird in the cage, they said to each other: 'There can be no doubt that if Malik Ibrahim brings this bird home, our father will make him his heir to the throne. It would be much better if we took the bird and handed him over in our own name.' Without any scruples they took the cage and continued their journey. Upon returning to their father, they placed the cage on the ground and told a few false stories which they had concocted about all the difficulties and dangers they had had to endure in order to gain possession of the bird. This gladdened the Sultan, he kissed his sons and begged them to sit down by his side. But the bird never opened his beak. Everyone present was surprised at the bird's refusal to chirp, and they went to see the physician who had advised that the bird be sought, telling him that they now had the bird but he would not sing. The physician said: 'Well this shows quite clearly that it was not the two princes who went to all that trouble to find the bird.' The physician's words were conveyed to the Sultan and he asked his vizier what he thought about it all. 'Yes,' said the vizier, 'I share the physician's view; it can only be Malik Ibrahim's doing.'

Meanwhile, Malik Ibrahim had woken up and when he saw that the cage had disappeared he knew at once who was responsible for its removal. He therefore rode into the city and went to his own abode. A short while later the vizier entered and said: 'Your father is asking for you.' Accompanied by the vizier, Malik Ibrahim went to see his father the king, kissed the ground before his feet as a token of respect, and arose. No sooner had the bird called Flower Trill become aware of Malik Ibrahim's presence than he started trilling merrily and the flowers began to drop from his beak. This proved to all present that it was Malik Ibrahim and not Malik Muhammad nor Malik Djamsheed who had brought the bird called Flower Trill. The Sultan kissed Malik Ibrahim on both cheeks, took off his crown and placed it upon Malik Ibrahim's head.

One month after this event, the scouts came and reported that a camp with magnificent tents had been established a few miles outside the city and that nobody knew whose camp it was. The Sultan ordered his vizier to ride out and investigate. The vizier set out and returned the next day with the following information: 'It is Tarfe Banu, the daughter of the Peri King of the Mountain of

Qaf, who has come to fetch her bird Flower Trill. She says she will talk to no one except the person who has robbed her of the bird.' Upon hearing this, all present turned pale, even the Sultan. What would she do with the prince? But Malik Ibrahim was of good cheer. 'I will go myself,' he said, 'to see what she intends to do.' He dressed in his finest clothes and rode out to where Tarfe Banu had pitched her tents.

When Tarfe Banu heard that the prince was coming, she said: 'Bring him into my tent!' He entered and Tarfe Banu rose, took his hand and bade him sit down by her side. 'Young hero,' she said, 'I swore that I would marry you; only a brave and courageous man who, like yourself, has successfully foiled the designs of all those witches and Peris and Divs and who has made himself master over the bird, is worthy of being my husband.' Delighted with the unexpected good fortune that had befallen him, Malik Ibrahim hurried home to his father and said: 'Prepare everything for the wedding!' The Sultan ordered the vizier to make all the necessary preparations for the ceremony, and the festivities in the city continued for a whole month.

Shortly afterwards, couriers were also despatched to Maimune Khatun, and they all lived in happiness and joy until the end of their days, as decreed by fate.

3. MUHAMMAD THE SHEPHERD AND THE PERI PRINCESSES

THERE once lived a shepherd called Muhammad, who dreamt one night that two stars appeared on his knees, and the moon on his chest. When he awoke, he thought to himself: 'I had better give up the life of a shepherd and go out into the world to find the meaning of my dream'; and so he arose and left the town.

He travelled for many nights and days until he reached an inn. He entered and lay down to sleep in a corner. As dawn broke he heard a voice calling his name. He opened his eyes and beheld a girl of indescribable beauty. 'Arise,' said the girl, 'and saddle the horse, so that we may continue our journey.' Muhammad rose, speechless with surprise, the girl mounted the horse and together they galloped away.

After the sun had risen, the girl looked at Muhammad and saw that he was not her servant after all. Greatly surprised, she asked who he was. He replied: 'I am a shepherd and I have set out to find the meaning of a dream I once had. When you called me I rose and went with you.'—'What did you dream?' she asked him. Muhammad told her of his dream, whereupon the girl said to him: 'I want you to know that I am the daughter of a Peri king and that I had the urge to travel. My servant's name also happens to be Muhammad. Last night we rested at that inn and this morning, when I called you, I thought you were my servant. Things have turned out differently, but if you are bright and quick I will be pleased to employ you in place of my servant.' To this Muhammad replied:

'I shall obey all your commands.'

So they travelled on until they reached a spring. There the girl dismounted for a meal. Meanwhile, Muhammad's attention was attracted by some pretty shining stones lying at the bottom of the spring. Without knowing what kind of stones they were, he picked up several of them and put them into his pocket. Later, they continued their journey. After riding for ten days and nights, they came to a town. The girl took up lodgings at a hostelry. After a few days she asked Muhammad: 'Have you still got the precious stones you took from the spring?' He replied: 'Which precious stones? I only know that I picked up a few pretty stones from the ground and put them into my pocket.'—'That is what I mean,' she said, 'show me the little stones.' Muhammad produced them; there were four. The girl took one and said: 'Take this gem as a present to the Sultan and then come back to me.'—'Your obedient servant,' replied Muhammad; he then dressed in suitable clothes, presented the precious stone to the Sultan and returned.

The Sultan was greatly surprised at the purity and beautiful colour of the stone. Although he was the ruler of a large country, he had never seen such a magnificent gem before. He said to his vizier: 'How could this peasant boy have come into the possession of so valuable a stone?' The vizier replied: 'According to what I have been able to find out, he also has with him an exquisite young girl whose beauty is unequalled by anyone on this earth. Such a beautiful girl is suitable for a Sultan and not for a peasant.'—'Vizier,' said the Sultan, 'give me some good advice on how to get rid of this young man so that I can become the girl's master.' The vizier replied: 'Your majesty, send for him and say: "I have forty wives; one of them has received the gem and now the others give her no peace. You must bring me another thirty-nine stones from the place where you found the first one, so that the quarrels may come to an end."' The Sultan immediately sent a servant to fetch Muhammad. When the young girl learned that the Sultan had sent for Muhammad, she realized at once that something important was happening. She therefore said to Muhammad: 'If the Sultan demands something of you, agree to it but ask for forty days' grace.'

So Muhammad went to see the Sultan who told him the false story about the forty wives and the one gem, and ordered him to obtain a further thirty-nine stones. Muhammad asked for forty days' grace and, on leaving, murmured to himself: 'I wish I had not taken those stones from the spring! I no longer have the faintest idea where that spring actually was.' When he returned to the hostelry and related how the king had demanded that he fetch the precious stones, the girl said to him: 'Do not worry about this. Just start on your journey right away. You will cross seven mountains and when you have reached the foot of the eighth, there you will find the spring, and then you must take thirty-nine of the gems, which you thought were pebbles, and return with them.'

Muhammad arose and went out. He crossed the seven mountains, reached the foot of the eighth and there, indeed, he found the spring. He sat down beside the spring and thought to himself: 'How strange that the little stones at the bottom of this spring are so beautiful and shining and that the king is so eager to have them!' And while he sat there and pondered on this, he saw a drop of blood fall from a tree above into the spring and turn into a precious stone. Muhammad looked up and, low and behold, there was a beautiful girl hanging in the tree. Her head had been cut off and from the wound fell the drops of blood which turned into gems that shone like lamps in the night.

He stood there, amazed, and regarded the strange scene. Suddenly he noticed a Div approaching at such speed that smoke issued from his nostrils as from a chimney. Muhammad, terribly afraid, hid himself and so became an eye-witness to strange events. The Div went towards the tree, climbed up, took out a book and began reading from it aloud. This caused the girl to sneeze; she climbed down, lively as a fish in the water, and sat on the ground. The Div pleaded with her: 'How much longer am I, miserable and poor wretch, expected to live without you!' To this the girl replied: 'And why did you drag me away from my father and my mother and my sisters to bring me here? Any love between us is out of the question.' All his urgent requests were in vain. Finally, the Div once again read out a few words from the book and the girl reverted to her previous state, whereupon he rose into the air, puffing like a chimney, and disappeared.

As soon as Muhammad had made sure that the Div had really gone, he crept from his hiding place, climbed up the tree and brought down the book. Then he started reading from it, as he had seen the Div do, and at the same instant the girl regained consciousness and came down from the tree. Upon seeing Muhammad she said: 'Young man, are you tired of living, to venture to this place? I want you to know that I am the daughter of the King of the Peris. This Div has fallen in love with me and has abducted me to this place. Seven years have now passed since he brought me here and during that time he has kept asking me to marry him, but I do not wish to have anything to do with him. He comes here once a week, but beg as he might he will never succeed; then he puts me into the state in which you saw me, and disappears to return a week later.'—'With God's help,' said Muhammad, 'I will arrange for you to escape. Next time the Div comes, you must be friendly to him and ask him nicely not to return you to the state of lifelessness.' The girl promised to follow his advice.

On the appointed day, the Div returned and, as usual, started to talk about his love for the girl. In reply, she said: 'This is a very strange manner of showing your love for me. I have been like a dead person for the last seven years. Stop depriving me of my consciousness and, who knows, perhaps love will gradually find its way to my heart.'—'I am at your service in any and every way,' the Div said joyfully. The next day, without reading from his book, he left the girl and flew away. No sooner had he disappeared than Muhammad stepped forward and went up to her. 'Next week,' he said, 'when the Div starts wooing you again, you must promise that you will marry him in forty days and then you must say to him: "I am so bored by myself. Give me the bottle which contains your soul so that it may afford me some company and entertainment."' The girl agreed to this suggestion.

So the week passed and again the Div appeared on the appointed day. The girl spoke to him tenderly: 'Yesterday I was so looking forward to today that I did not know what to do with myself.'—'My beloved,' said the Div, 'if you promise to marry me, I will almost die with happiness.'—'The wedding shall take place in forty days,' replied the girl. The Div was beside himself with joy and could not do enough to please her. When the girl saw that he was intoxicated with love, she chose the right moment and said to him: 'During all the days I have to spend here, I feel so terribly lonely. Give me the bottle in which you keep your soul, so that it may entertain me in my solitude.' As soon as the Div heard these words, he flew into a rage and struck the girl's face so hard that she fell down in a faint. But immediately afterwards he took pity on her and revived her. 'Look,' he said in a loving voice, 'under that stone slab there is a well and in the well the bottle containing my soul is suspended from a hair. It is simply impossible to remove it from there to give to you.' —'Very well,' said the girl, 'in that case let this stone slab keep me company.'

The Div eventually flew away and Muhammad and the girl went over to the stone slab. I am unable to recall how it came about, but finally they managed to push the slab aside. Muhammad climbed down into the well and spread out his coat, at the same time holding the bottle, and he then called up to the girl that she could now cut the strand of hair. The girl cut it and the bottle fell into Muhammad's outspread coat. He picked it up and climbed out of the well.

After another seven days had passed, the Div returned. This time, however, Muhammad did not crawl into his hiding place. When the Div saw Muhammad, he roared: 'How dare you appear here, wretched human being! Now your mother shall join you to bewail your death!' He grasped the tree, tore it out at its roots and was about to attack Muhammad. Suddenly, upon approaching more closely and seeing that Muhammad held the bottle containing the Div's soul in his hand, the Div began to shake, threw away the tree and pleaded: 'Give me back the bottle with my soul and I will be your slave until the day you die, and do everything you order me to do.' Muhammad told him: 'Take me and this young girl and carry us into the town; then you can take your bottle and run away wherever you wish.' The Div replied: 'I will obey all your commands.' Muhammad picked up all the gems in the spring and sat down on the Div's back together with the girl. The Div rose high into the air and they flew away. On reaching the town, the Div descended and asked for his bottle, but Muhammad smashed it on to the ground whereupon the Div turned into smoke and disappeared.

Muhammad and his companion went into the town and took up lodgings at the inn. When the two girls, who were sisters, saw each other, they embraced and thanked Muhammad with all their hearts for having brought about their reunion.

The next morning Muhammad took the gems to the Sultan, who had certainly never expected to see him again. Greatly surprised, he took the precious stones and allowed Muhammad to go. He then said to his vizier: 'See if you can invent some way of getting rid of this troublesome young man, because I am almost dying of love for the girl.'—'My informers tell me,' replied the vizier, 'that Muhammad has brought back a girl from his last journey who is even more beautiful than the first one.'—'I do not care,' said the king, 'you must send him to a place from which he can never return.' The vizier thought for a while and then said: 'Tell him to bring us the red roses from the tree which grows in the country of the man-eating Divs; it is absolutely impossible for him to come back from there.' And so they sent for Muhammad and the Sultan said to him: 'I must have a few red roses from the Divs' tree. Go forth and bring them to me. I will not hear of any excuses or pretexts.' Once again Muhammad asked for forty days' grace and returned to the inn. He told the two girls what had happened. 'You need not worry about this at all,' they said to him, 'you will have no difficulty whatever in obtaining the red roses.' The girl whom he had freed last continued: 'Return to the same spring. From there count four mountains on your right and when you come to the fifth, you will meet an old man. Greet him and say that you have come to find the red roses. All you have to do then is to follow the old man's instructions.'

Equipped with these directions, Muhammad once again started on his journey. He reached the spring, counted four mountains on his right and at the fifth he met an old man of magnificent appearance who was saying his prayers. Muhammad greeted him and informed him that he had come to find the red roses. The old man said: 'Go and kill a fat sheep and divide it into two halves.' Muhammad did as he was told. Then the old man said to him: 'Take the meat and go to the foot of that mountain over there. On your left you will see a garden in which live thousands of man-eating Divs. Creep into the garden very carefully. All the Divs will be lying there fast asleep. They wake up only once a week and fortunately today is the first day of their week's sleep. Go in and pass through their midst until you reach a building with two huge dogs chained at the entrance. Throw half a sheep to each of the two dogs, hurry into the house, pick up a white bundle lying there and escape as fast as you can. But take care not to step on any of those Divs while you are running, because if they wake up they will eat you up in one gulp.'

Muhammad did exactly as the old man instructed, took the white bundle and brought it to him. 'In this bundle,' said the old man, 'there is a young girl, the sister of the two who have sent you here. Take her to her sisters. After she has regained consciousness, bleed her at her right hand

and each drop of blood falling from her hand will turn into a red rose.'

Muhammad started his journey in good spirits. After several days of travelling he arrived at the inn again and handed the bundle to the two sisters. They opened it, brought their sister back to life and embraced her warmly. Then they bled their sister, collected the blood in a bowl, and each drop turned into a red rose. They placed all the roses in a dish and had them brought before the king.

When the Sultan saw Muhammad and the dish of roses, he turned to the vizier and said: 'This is terrible! Even if we send this man straight to Hell, he will still return safely!'—'Your majesty may rest assured,' replied the vizier, 'this time I will send him somewhere else and even if he had a thousand lives, he would not be able to save a single one of them.'—'And where is he to be sent this time?' asked the Sultan. The vizier replied: 'I will send him to the mare with the forty foals. Nobody has so far been able to accomplish this mission.' This satisfied the Sultan and he then said to Muhammad: 'I am truly delighted that you have brought me the red roses; but I have one more wish, which is that you go and fetch me the mare with the forty foals.' Muhammad raised no objection and asked only for forty days' grace. Then he went back to the inn and said to the sisters: 'Now the Sultan wants the mare with the forty foals and he has given me forty days to fetch them. What shall I do?'

The third sister said: 'Let me solve this problem for you. Take ten loads of sugar, one large mirror, one saddle, a set of jewel-studded reins and forty oranges. With these things go into the forest where the mare with the forty foals is living. First you must pour the ten loads of sugar into the spring of bitter water which flows there. Put the mirror up against a tree opposite the spring. Place the saddle and the reins next to the mirror. Then climb up the tree. When the mare with the forty foals comes to the spring and drinks from the water, she will say "Oh, how sweet the water tastes!" Then she will look at herself in the mirror and say: "Oh dear, how I have aged! How wonderful it would be if someone came and brushed my coat!" To this you reply: "I shall be glad to do this." Then you must climb down from the tree and brush her coat. When she sees the saddle and reins she will say: "How pleased I should be if someone were to place the saddle on my back!" "I shall be glad to do this," will be your reply. And when you have saddled her and put on the reins, she will again look into the mirror and say: "Look how young I have become! It would be a real treat for me if someone were to jump on my back and we were to gallop about!" You must climb into the saddle at once. Later, when she asks you to dismount after the ride, take no notice. She will then start neighing to call her foals so that they may come and tear you to pieces, but you must simply throw an orange into the mouth of each of them. This will blunt their teeth so that they cannot do you any harm. Then you must gallop away and take the mare with the forty foals straight to the Sultan's stables.'

Muhammad followed these excellent instructions and brought the mare and the forty foals into the Sultan's stables. The Sultan and the vizier certainly could not complain about this, but now they simply did not know what to do. However, after thinking for a while the vizier said: 'Wherever we may send that man in this world, he will always return alive. Therefore, there is only one solution to this problem: we must send him into the next world.'—'How are we to accomplish that?' asked the king.

'In this way, your majesty,' said the vizier, 'write a letter to your late father and require Muhammad to deliver the letter and return with the reply.' So the king summoned Muhammad, gave him the letter he had written and said: 'Since the death of the Sultan, my father, I have been without news from him. I am convinced that you will be able to put this right. This is definitely the last wish I want you to fulfil.'

The unfortunate Muhammad had no choice but to accept this task too. He went back to the three girls and showed them the Sultan's letter. 'Do not worry,' they said, 'go straight to the Sultan and say to him: "Tomorrow give orders for ten donkey-loads of wood to be taken outside the city and stacked there; then place me in the centre of that pile of wood. The wood is then to be set alight, so that I can move on into the next world and collect the Sultan's reply."' With these instructions, Muhammad went to see the Sultan. The Sultan and the vizier were pleased, and the vizier ordered ten donkey-loads of wood to be taken outside the city and stacked there. Then he ordered the town crier to inform all the inhabitants that they must assemble to witness the spectacle.

Next morning, Muhammad went to the appointed place, carrying the letter with the Sultan's seal. All the inhabitants had gathered to enjoy this unusual display. Muhammad sat on top of the pile and then the wood was set alight. When the flames began to spread and the wood surrounding Muhammad started burning, the girls turned themselves into eagles, seized Muhammad and removed him, unseen, from the flames. When the fire had spent itself, the Sultan and the vizier returned to the castle, highly satisfied.

Forty days went by and the Sultan said to his vizier:

'The agreed time ends today; this time Muhammad will not come back, that is absolutely certain. Tomorrow I shall send out my men and have the girls brought into my harem.' Before the Sultan could finish speaking, Muhammad, his head and face black with ash, entered and placed a sealed letter at the Sultan's feet. On seeing Muhammad, the Sultan could hardly believe his eyes. He stood there speechless for a long time. When his rage had abated a little, he took the letter and looked at it. There could be no doubt that his father's handwriting and seal were genuine. At last he opened the letter and read: 'Your letter was brought to me by Muhammad and pleased me greatly. I am going to give a banquet within the next few days, and without your company and that of your vizier, our pleasure would not be complete. You can come to us by the same means as Muhammad and return later.' The king examined the letter in the minutest detail. It was his father's handwriting. Then he asked Muhammad: 'How did you feel in the midst of all the flames?'—'I did not notice anything,' he replied. 'I only lost consciousness and when I awoke and opened my eyes, I found myself in the next world. And what a world it is! No one can imagine all that splendour unless he has seen it with his own eyes. His majesty, the late Sultan, sat on the highest fortress of the paradise and the late Grand Vizier was also there.'

In short, he described everything so vividly that the Sultan, too, became anxious to see the next world. So the Sultan and his vizier travelled into the next world along the route by which they had despatched Muhammad. But they never returned, although the Sultan had said to his courtiers that he would be back before forty days had passed. The forty days went by, but there was no sign of the Sultan nor of his vizier. Two months, then three months passed; the country had no ruler and there was chaos everywhere. At long last the people abandoned all hope of the Sultan's returning, and by a large majority they elected Muhammad as their king. After Muhammad had come to power in this manner, he married the three girls, sat one of them on his right knee, the second on his left, and the third was given her place between the other two.

4. THE BLACK FOAL

THERE once lived a king who had a fourteen-year-old son. The boy's mother had died when he was three years old and the king had married again, but the boy's stepmother disliked him so much that she could not bear the sight of him. The prince happened to possess a black foal which he loved beyond measure. The first thing he did every morning before going to school, and after coming home in the evening, was to go and see his foal, stroke it and give it sweets. The stepmother, who resented the prince's love for the black foal, planned to harm the animal and thereby hurt the boy. She gave a large sum of money to one of her slave girls whom she trusted and said to her: 'Go to all the physicians in the town, give them money and tell them that if they are called to the king's harem to see the queen, every one of them must prescribe the meat of the black foal as a remedy.' She then dissolved a little yellowroot in water and painted it all over her body, placed some dry bread in a piece of cloth which she tied around herself, and then she took to her bed.

When the sultan heard that his wife was ill, he went to the harem at once. There she lay on her sickbed, looking as yellow as if she had been suffering from jaundice for a whole year, and each time she moved, the dry bread made a crunching sound and she cried out: 'Oh, my ribs! I feel as if my loins were bursting.' The king immediately gave orders for the physicians to be summoned. They came and examined the patient most carefully and were unanimous in prescribing for her the meat of the black foal. The king, who knew how much his son loved the black foal, sank into deep thought. He could not bring himself to hurt the feelings of his only son and heir by allowing the black foal to be killed, but on the other hand the physicians insisted that the foal would have to be slaughtered because that was the only way of helping the sick queen. At last the king agreed, and said: 'Very well, tomorrow the prince's teachers shall be ordered to keep him at school all day.' In view of the fact that the prince loved his foal so dearly, the king did not want him to be present at the slaughter of his favourite pet.

In the afternoon, when the prince went to see his foal as usual, he noticed that it was shedding bitter tears and refusing all food. He kissed the foal and stroked it, and asked what had happened. The foal replied: 'Your step-mother hates me because of your love for me and now she pretends to be ill; she has bribed the physicians to declare that my meat is the only remedy which could cure her. It has therefore been decided that I am to be killed at noon tomorrow, and your teachers have been ordered to keep you at school all day long. So our signal will be this: When I neigh the first time, it means that they are dragging me out; when I neigh the second time, it is to let you know that they are tying my legs, and when you hear me neighing the third time, please come and rescue me; otherwise they will cut off my head. If you do succeed in reaching me before it is too late, jump on to my back and I will fly away with you.' The prince replied: 'Do not worry, whatever may happen I will come to you.'

Next morning the prince went to school and performed his duties. Suddenly he heard his foal neigh. He rose and said to the teacher: 'Please, Sir, may I go?'—'Sit down!' said the teacher harshly. Shortly afterwards they heard neighing for the second time, whereupon the prince rose again, saying: 'Please, Sir, may I go now?' The teacher, however, beat him with a cane and made him sit down. A short while later, when the boy heard his foal neighing for the third time, he again asked for permission to leave. The teacher approached, brandishing a cane and trying to force the prince to sit down, but the boy took a bowl full of red-hot charcoal and threw it at the teacher's head, then he took a handful of coins from his pocket and scattered them among the other boys. While they were busy picking up the money, he rushed out through the door and ran home. There, he threw himself over the foal, crying, and although his father spoke kindly to him and promised him all sorts of things, it was to no avail. The prince said: 'Surely it would not be unreasonable if I asked for permission to ride my foal for the last time? If I am to agree to my foal being killed, I wish him first to be saddled, and a saddle big filled with gems and money placed across his back and then I want to ride round the courtyard three times. After that, you may kill the foal.'—'All right,' said the sultan, 'I have no objections,' and he gave orders for a bag filled with jewels and coins and a gem-studded saddle cloth to be placed on the foal's back, and for the prince to be lifted into the saddle. The prince rode twice round the courtyard and the third time the foal rose high up into the sky and disappeared from everybody's view, leaving the sultan and the others standing there gaping, not knowing what to do next.

Meanwhile, the foal had risen so high that the prince lost sight of the earth below. He then ordered the foal to descend. The foal set him down in a garden in a strange country, gave him a few hairs from his coat and said: 'If you find yourself in any kind of trouble, simply throw one of these hairs into the fire and I shall come to you at once, because I belong to the family of the Peris.' And with these words the foal disappeared.

The prince concealed his coat and jewels in a corner and, taking only one single coin with him, went into the hut of a Kallepazi[1]. There, he took a sheep's bladder and pulled it over his head so that he looked as if he were bald. He then went up to a kind old gardener and asked him: 'Gentle Sir, have you any use for the services of an apprentice?'—'Yes,' replied the gardener, 'I have.' The prince said: 'Just give me my daily bread, that is all I ask.' The old man agreed and explained: 'This garden belongs to the king. He has seven daughters all of whom live here. This means that you must always be on your best behaviour, otherwise they will be cross with you, which God forbid, because then you would have reason to regret it.'—'You need have no fear,' said the prince. Every morning the gardener made up seven bunches of flowers and took them to the sultan's daughters. One day the prince said to him: 'Do let me tie the bunches of flowers today.' And so the old man left that duty to his apprentice, who made up seven beautiful bunches and handed them to the gardener. When he took them to the princesses, they said: 'Listen, old man, you never tied these bunches yourself, so tell us who did.' He replied: 'I have a young apprentice who has been helping me for the past few days. It was he who tied these bunches.'—'Go and bring him here,' they told him. The old man obeyed and brought the prince along and the princesses said: 'From today onwards, this young man shall tie our bunches of flowers!' But the youngest princess was very shrewd. She looked at the prince a little more closely and found it difficult to believe that he really was a young gardener. Then the gardener and the boy were allowed to go.

Some time passed. At noon on a terribly hot day the prince thought. 'I am sure everybody in the garden will be asleep now. I will refresh myself a little.' Immediately behind the palace of the princesses there flowed a small river. First, the prince took a hair of the black foal and burnt it. The foal appeared at once. The prince then removed the sheep's bladder from his head and bathed in the river, without noticing that the youngest of the princesses was watching him from a palace window. After he had bathed, the prince put on his royal robes, saddled the foal, mounted and rode along the outside wall of the garden several times. The princess observed everything and was most impressed with the prince's handsome appearance. Meanwhile, the prince had dismounted, put on his old clothes once again and replaced the skin bladder on his head, whereupon the foal disappeared.

A few days later the princesses were sitting together, talking. The eldest said: 'Why does father not make arrangements for us to be married?' One of them suggested: 'We shall probably have to take matters into our own hands.'—'But how are we going to do that?' asked the others. She replied: 'I know what we must do.' They ordered seven fully ripened melons to be brought to them, and each princess pushed her knife into a melon; they then sent the seven melons to the sultan. He was unable to understand the meaning of this and asked his vizier if he did. The vizier replied: 'It simply means: "We are fully ripened, just like these melons and are waiting for a husband."'—'Very well,' said the sultan, 'in that case order the criers to announce throughout the town that all eligible men, whether of high or low rank, are required to assemble at a certain place on a given day. Moreover, see to it that my daughters are given seven oranges; each must throw her orange to the man she has chosen.'

The town crier carried out his orders and on the appointed day all the men, from the highest to the most humble, appeared at the specified place. Each princess threw her orange to the man of her choice, one to the vizier's son, another to the Emir's son, while each of the others chose the son of a prince—all, that is, except the youngest princess. She looked in all directions for the gardener's apprentice but was unable to discover him anywhere and just stood there, holding her orange. This angered the sultan and he ordered the entire town to be searched for any remaining men. His servants searched everywhere but could find only a bald-headed youth who was busy watering the flowers in the princesses' garden. 'Come with us,' the servants told him, 'on the sultan's orders.' The bald-headed youth scratched the back of his head and burst into tears. 'But I have not done anything,' he said. The servants, however, paid no attention whatever, grabbed him by the scruff of his neck and dragged him along. As soon as the princess saw the boy she loved, she flung the orange at him, which struck him squarely on the head. He pretended to cry and said: 'Oh, my poor head!' When the people around him saw this, they started threatening him and shouted: 'You miserable lout, you should go down on your knees and thank God for having won the love of the sultan's daughter!' The sultan, however, was extremely angry about his daughter having made such an unsuitable choice and said: 'From today, I will no longer regard her as my daughter. For all I care, she and her husband can do as they like.' And he ordered the princess to be banished from the royal castle. She, however, did not mind in the least because she knew that her husband was a prince who had deliberately disguised himself. Holding hands, they went off and bought a small house outside the town, where they lived together in happiness.

One day the sultan fell ill. The physicians prescribed for him a special broth made with gazelle meat. Thereupon the sultan's sons-in-law engaged hunters and went to the hunting grounds to shoot gazelles. The prince also heard about this. He burnt a foal's hair at once and said to the foal, which had appeared immediately: 'I wish to go hunting. Provide me with everything needed for a royal hunt and tell the Peris to drive together near my camp all the gazelles which are normally to be found in the mountains around the town.' The black foal obeyed and carried out the prince's orders at once; the prince mounted the foal and rode out to the hunt. He then made himself comfortable in his tent.

The king's sons-in-law and their huntsmen rode all through the mountains for two or three days without finding any trace of the game and, greatly surprised, they asked themselves where all the gazelles could have gone. Finally, their hounds picked up a trail which led them straight to the prince's camp. Near the royal tents they saw thousands of gazelles gathered together like a flock of sheep. The master of the camp was evidently a very high-ranking young nobleman. The sons-in-law approached politely and asked him if he might let them have a few gazelles. 'We are the sultan's sons-in-law,' they said. 'The sultan has fallen sick and the physicians have prescribed for him a broth made of gazelle meat. We have been riding in the mountains and the plains for many days searching for gazelles, but we have been unable to find even one. If you could let us have a few of these gazelles, you would indeed be doing us a great favour.'—'Yes,' replied the prince, 'I will give you a few, but on one condition only.' —'And what is that condition?' He replied: 'That I brand you on the back with my slave mark before giving you one gazelle carcass each; but I shall keep the heads for myself.' At first they refused to accept his terms, but seeing that he was adamant, they had to submit whether they liked it or not. And so he branded each of them with the mark that was usually applied to the heads of his cattle. Then he cut off the gazelles' heads, thinking to himself: 'The king's health does, after all, depend on the heads alone.' Each man was given his gazelle carcass, and the prince let them go.

The sons-in-law handed the gazelle carcasses to the cook who prepared a broth from them which was served to the sultan, but it had no effect whatsoever. In the meantime, the prince had sent the black foal away. He then placed the gazelle heads into a basket, which he tied to the back of an ass, and entered the town, wearing his tattered clothes and the skin bladder on his head. When the sons-in-law saw the bald young man with the gazelle heads, they laughed and ridiculed him: 'Look at him, he also wants to cook a broth for the king!' The prince, however, took no notice. He calmly continued along the road and when he reached his house near the town, he gave the heads to his wife and said: 'Hurry, take these heads and make a broth from them. This should then be taken to your father so that he may be healed.' The princess prepared the broth and sent it to her father. The sultan, however, was furious when he saw his daughter's messenger but his wife, the princess's mother, tried to make him more charitable by saying: 'Do remember, the girl is your daughter, after all, and she has the best of intentions. Surely there is no harm in your trying a little of the broth, if only so as not to hurt her feelings; has she not prepared the broth with her own hands? Besides, who knows, it might even restore your health.' The sultan calmed down and tried a few spoonfuls of the broth. He enjoyed it very much and his pain eased. He felt much better, and decided to treat his daughter more kindly in future.

A week went by, and the king's scouts came to report that a number of princely tents had been erected about a mile outside the town, but that nobody knew who owned them. The king sent for his vizier and told him: 'Find out to whom those tents belong and what has brought the stranger here.' The vizier went out and when he returned he told the sultan: 'He is a noble prince who has come here to search for six escaped slaves. He claims that they are living at the sultan's court and that all six bear his mark burnt on their backs.' The sultan, accompanied by all his courtiers, went out to the prince who gave him a most magnificent reception, which greatly impressed and surprised the sultan. The prince said to him: 'None of these men are my slaves.' Astonished, the sultan replied: 'There is no one else at my court except my six sons-in-law.' He gave orders for them to be summoned. The moment they entered, the prince called out: 'Here they are! These are my slaves and if you do not believe me, all you have to do is to bare their backs.' Their shirts were pulled down and to everyone's surprise, the brands on their backs were revealed. There the unhappy sons-in-law of the sultan stood, shamefacedly and with their eyes downcast, unable to utter a word.

At that moment, the sultan's daughter emerged from behind a curtain, embraced her father and said: 'That young man over there is my master and husband.' And then she told her father the whole story. The sultan kissed the young prince on both cheeks, took off his crown and placed it upon the prince's head.

5. THE BALD HERDSMAN

ONCE upon a time there lived a bald man who made his living by driving other people's cattle to the pastures. In the morning he drove the cows belonging to the villagers out into the fields, and in the evening he brought them back, receiving something for his labour from each of the owners. One day, the mayor's daughter happened to come along to fill her pitcher with water. The bald man immediately fell in love with her a thousand times over. The girl said to him: 'Come and lift the pitcher on to my shoulder.' This pleased the bald man; he placed the pitcher on her shoulder and was rewarded with a kiss. The young girl went home and said to her mother: 'Today I met a bald-headed man who came along with a few oxen and did this and that.' Her mother happened to be an understanding woman and said: 'My dear child, one does not do such a thing.'

When the bald man returned to the village from the pastures that evening he first took the animals back to their owners and then went to his mother and said to her: 'Mother dear, I want to marry the mayor's daughter and you must go to her parents and ask for their daughter's hand on my behalf.' His mother tried to reason with him, putting forward every possible argument: 'Don't forget, my boy, the girl is the mayor's daughter and we are poor folk without a penny to our name.' The bald man, however, would not listen to her objections and said: 'At daybreak tomorrow you must go and court the mayor's daughter for me.'—'All right then, I will go,' the poor woman replied, 'let us see what tomorrow brings.'

In the yard of the mayor's house there was a stone, and anyone looking for a bride had to sit on that stone so that the people could see that he wanted to find a wife[1]. At dawn, after the bald man had driven the cattle out to graze, his mother went to the mayor's house and sat down on the stone. The mayor's wife, who was a shrewd woman, understood the other woman's intentions quite clearly. She thought: 'Yesterday the baldhead kissed my daughter and today his mother is here to ask her hand on his behalf.' She turned to her slave and said to her: 'If there is anything left over from last night's supper, take a small portion out to the baldhead's mother, and also give her two qran and send her away.' The slave girl gave the bald man's mother some food and the money. The mother felt too embarrassed to say anything, so she kept quiet that day and went home.

At sunset the bald man returned home. 'Well, mother,' he asked, 'did you go there?' His mother again started to argue with him: 'Quite frankly, we are only a couple of poor devils and the best thing you can do is to get these ideas right out of your head. I will gladly ask for the hand of your uncle's daughter.' At this, however, the bald man picked up a stick and threatened his mother: 'If you don't go out at dawn tomorrow and fix up my engagement to the mayor's daughter, I will beat you.' And so his mother was forced to give in and to promise to go out at daybreak and make sure by some means or other that the girl would become his. So, at the crack of dawn, the woman went once again to the mayor's courtyard, sat down on the stone and presented her request. The mayor's wife said to her: 'I will speak on your behalf and support your request, but I shall have to leave the final decision to the mayor.'

When the mayor came home in the evening, his wife told him what had happened: 'You just sit here, quite calmly, while the bald-headed herdsman has fallen in love with your daughter! His mother was here today to ask for her hand in marriage, and I promised to do my best for her.' The mayor, who was an honest and decent man, said: 'We all know that the poor fellow is penniless, he has neither a house nor a livelihood. I do not wish to reject him outright but I want to tell him to go and earn some money first and set up house. Then he can have the girl.'

This decision was conveyed to the bald man who was very pleased about it. That day he did not take the cows out to graze but only said to his mother: 'I shall go now and try to get some money.' She begged him to abandon the idea: 'Do not leave your mother here on her own. Where do you want to go? Stay here and trust in God.'—'No,' he replied, 'I cannot do that.' Then he turned his back on his native village and went out into the desert. He travelled from one place to another until one day he met a dervish. 'Listen, baldhead,' said the dervish, 'where are you going? Are you looking for work?'—'Yes, I am.'—'How much do you want as a daily wage?—'Whatever you are willing to give me.'—'In that case let us go,' said the dervish.

They walked and walked until at last they reached a well filled with water. 'Let us have some food and drink here,' said the dervish. They sat down, ate bread and drank water; then the dervish said: 'Wait here, baldhead, while I go home; I shall be back soon.' The bald man noticed that the dervish said a few magic words and then climbed into the well, where he disappeared. A short while later he came up again and said: 'Come, let us go.'—'Where are we going?' the bald man asked.

The dervish told him to close his eyes, taught him how to pronounce the Almighty's name and said: 'Now come with me.' The bald man pronounced the magic word and they both descended into the well. When he opened his eyes again, he found himself in a beautiful garden. He had never seen such a wonderful place in all his life. 'Have a good look round,' said the dervish, 'and follow me wherever I go.' Together, they entered a summer house. There he saw a girl who was as beautiful as the moon of the fourteenth night[2]. The dervish left the bald man in the care of the girl, who was his daughter, gave her a book and said to her: 'I am going hunting and I shall return in forty days' time. Meanwhile you must instruct the baldhead in the art of reading this book.'—'Very well,' said the daughter, and the dervish went away.

The girl taught the bald man to read the book. But then she said to him: 'If my father finds out that you have learned what is written in this book, he will bring misfortune upon your head.'—'Well,' said the bald man, 'what am I to do?' The girl replied: 'When my father comes back and asks you whether you are able to read the book, you must reply: "Yes." But when he starts testing you and wants you to say "A", for example, you must say "B". You must read everything the wrong way round so that he will think you have understood nothing.'

After the forty days were over, there was a puffing and blowing in the air as if from a chimney, and the dervish arrived. He turned to his daughter and asked: 'Has the baldhead read the book?'—'I must say, he is indeed a strange fellow,' replied the daughter, 'no matter what he is supposed to read, he does not understand one jot.' The dervish pointed to the letter 'A' and asked him: 'What is this letter?' 'This is "B",' replied the bald man. The dervish pointed to one word and then another, but it was no use—the bald man did not understand anything. Thereupon the dervish said to his daughter: 'This fellow is of no use to us. Fetch me a bag of money; I will give it to him and send him away.' He then gave the bald man fifty toman and said: 'You may go in peace, we have no use for you.'

Now the reader ought to know that the book was a magic one. Everything between heaven and earth was to be found in it, and the bald man had learnt it all. He returned to his mother and said: 'Look, mother, here is some money! Send for the builder and the masons and tell them to build a house. If the money is not enough, I will get some more.' The builder and the masons came and the bald man modelled the design of his new house on the one he had seen in the garden of the dervish.

In the evening he said to his mother: 'Listen, mother dear, tomorrow morning I shall turn myself into a camel. You must take me by the halter and lead me into the town; there you must sell me for a hundred toman. But the halter is not for sale and you must not part with it, even if they offer you a thousand toman for it.' In the morning, the mother took the bald man, who had turned himself into a camel, by the halter and led him to the market in the town. She sold the camel for one hundred toman and took the halter back with her. In the evening, as the sun disappeared behind the mountains, the old woman saw the bald man returning home. 'Pay the builder the hundred toman,' he told her. And later that evening he said to his mother: 'Next time, mother dear, I am going to turn myself into a mule at dawn. You must take me to the bazaar and sell me for one thousand toman, but you must not sell the halter with me.' Early next morning, before the sun had fully risen, the old woman took the bald man, who had assumed the shape of a mule, to the bazaar. At that moment a merchant passed by on his way from the baths. He admired the beautiful mule and asked the price. 'One thousand toman,' said the old woman. 'Listen to me, mother,' said the merchant, 'may the Lord have mercy upon your father! I have a hundred mules which I bought for thirty to forty toman each. It is true that yours is a particularly fine-looking mule and this is why I am willing to pay you one hundred toman for it, but a thousand toman is really too much.'—'Noble Sir,' the old woman protested, 'I want you to know that in actual fact my mule is worth two thousand toman. It is able to speed to any place on earth and return with a message within the hour.'—'How is that possible!' exclaimed the merchant. 'If that is true, I will gladly pay you two thousand toman instead of a thousand.'—'Why not put it to the test,' said the old woman.

The merchant took the old woman and the mule along to his house and told her that if the mule were able to run to the city of Rome and back within one hour, he would pay her two thousand toman. The reason was that he had a brother in Rome and wanted to know how he was keeping. He asked the woman to make an omelette at once, while he wrote a letter. Then he placed the omelette into a metal dish which he sealed and, after having sealed the letter as well, he handed both to his servant with these instructions: 'Mount the mule; it is supposed to take you to Rome and back within the hour.' The servant had hardly time to make himself comfortable in the saddle before he found himself in a strange city. 'What is the name of this place?' he asked. 'You are in Rome,' the people told him. 'And where can I find a certain inn?' He was shown the way to the inn and entered the room of the merchant's brother and gave him the letter. The other merchant saw that it was written only a short while ago. 'Servant,' he said, 'what else have you brought?' The servant handed him the omelette, which was still hot. The man ate it, wrote a letter in reply and handed it to the servant who once again mounted his mule and returned to the bazaar of his native town. His master, the merchant, was completely beside himself with surprise. He gave his servant a large amount of money to stop him from telling anyone about the fabulous mule he now owned, and to the old woman he said: 'Well, my dear, you wanted a thousand toman for this mule; I will now give you an extra five hundred.' The old woman took the money and went home, while the merchant told his servant to spread a carpet under the mule and to feed it with sugar and confectionery instead of hay and clover. After a few days had past, the merchant's wife said to him: 'May misfortune befall you! When you have at long last acquired such a splendid mule, why don't you look after it yourself?'—'You are quite right,' replied the merchant, 'I shall go down first thing tomorrow morning to see how the animal is getting along.' Next morning he went down to the stables. It was a pure joy to see the mule's coat shining like a peacock! Allah be praised! He scratched the mule's head and ears. But what was happening? The mule stood there and put his mouth into a hole in the wall. The merchant turned to his servant and asked him: 'Did you brush the mule's coat?'—'But of course,' replied the servant, 'I did brush the mule.' And then the merchant saw the animal's mouth becoming thinner and thinner until it began to disappear. What the devil was the matter with the mule? Next, they saw the mule's head disappear. There is no God but Allah!

Something very mysterious was going on here! And now even the neck disappeared. 'Help! Help! What a diabolical animal!' They saw the body disappear. 'Servant, hold on tightly!' Would you believe it, now the entire mule disappeared into the wall. They held on to its tail but it came off and the hole closed. 'Servant, break down the wall!' The servant replied: 'I am not a mason. But I advise you, master, not to tell anyone what has happened here, otherwise people will think you have gone mad.' The merchant gave his servant five hundred toman so that he would keep quiet about the whole affair.

The bald man's mother, however, was very worried when she did not see him for two or three days. But one fine day, she turned round to see him coming towards her, smiling cheerfully. 'My child,' she said, 'I would glady have sacrificed myself for you! Where have you been all this time? My heart was heavy with worry for you. But now your house is completed.'—'Mother, dear,' said the bald man, 'tomorrow morning I shall turn myself into a ram. You will take me to the bazaar and sell me for twenty toman, but you must not sell the chain I shall be wearing round my neck.'

Early next morning the old woman put the ram on a chain and led him to the bazaar. Just as she was about to cross the open market square, the dervish appeared suddenly. At this, the ram started shaking like a leaf. 'This is a very tricky situation,' he thought, 'dust and ashes upon my head! The dervish will tear me into a thousand pieces.' The dervish approached the old woman and said: 'I say, old woman, how much do you want for this ram?'—'Twenty toman,' she replied.—'Here are twenty toman,' he said, 'and now give me the chain.' The old woman replied: 'I am selling only the ram, not the chain.'—'I am willing to give you twenty toman for the chain.'—'No, I am not selling the chain.'—'But why not?' Meanwhile, people had begun to gather around them. 'Listen, old woman, the chain is not even worth a qran.' And they kept on talking to her until they persuaded her to sell the chain, too. And so the dervish took the ram together with the chain. How he longed for revenge! He dragged the ram as far as the well, descended with it and entered the house. Then he called his daughter: 'You close-cropped hussy[3]! You lied to me. You and this cursed baldhead put your heads together and tried to trick me. You taught him my art, but now I shall teach you both something else. Go and fetch the knife!' The girl went away but instead of bringing the knife she came back with a water jug. The dervish shouted: 'I told you to fetch the knife!' The daughter went and returned with a wine vessel. And each time he ordered his daughter to fetch the knife, she brought him something else instead. Finally, he lost his temper and released the ram's chain to fetch the knife himself. At that moment the ram turned itself into a dove and flew high up into the sky. The dervish turned himself into a falcon and pursued the dove. Both birds flapped their wings and flew as fast as they could, the dove in front and the falcon closely behind. The falcon almost caught the dove, but at that instant the dove became a bunch of flowers and dropped into the lap of a merchant's daughter who happened to be sitting at the edge of a pool near her house.

The falcon transformed itself back into a dervish. He approached the doorstep of the house and called out: 'Oh Lord! May Ali come to my aid! The flowers which have just dropped into this young girl's lap are mine.'—'All right,' replied the girl, 'here, take these hundred toman, father dervish, and the flowers will be mine.'—'That is out of the question,' said the dervish, and no matter how much he was offered for the flowers, he simply refused to sell them. Finally, the girl lost patience and threw the flowers at the dervish. The flowers, however, turned at once into a bushel of millet scattered over the house and garden. The dervish turned himself into a hen with chicks, which started pecking up the millet grains, but one of the grains had dropped between some petals and try as it might, the hen was unable to find it.

While all this was going on, the people and servants of the house stood around and watched the spectacle. They were speechless with surprise at these mysterious happenings. Suddenly, the grain of millet, which had lain hidden between the petals, turned into a fox which grabbed the hen and the chicks and gobbled them up.

At this the merchant called out: 'Catch the fox!' They caught him and said to him: 'In the name of the Lord who has created you in this shape, explain to us the secrets of all that has happened here.'

On hearing this, the fox turned into our old friend, the bald man, and he told them the whole story from A to Z, starting from the days when he used to drive the cattle to the pastures; he told them what he had seen in the house of the dervish and of everything that had happened as a result of the art he had learnt from the dervish's daughter. Later, he was able to marry the mayor's daughter, whom he loved so passionately, and so all the bald-headed herdsman's dreams came true.

6. THE FALSE CHIEF RAMMAL

THERE once lived a man and his wife: the husband was very poor, but his wife was so beautiful she was able to say to the moon: 'When I am here, you may just as well stay away.' For two months the poor man had not earned enough to give his wife ten shahi to go to the baths. She grumbled and said: 'A fine husband who cannot find even ten shahi so that his wife can visit the baths!' After several days, he at last managed to save up ten shahi to enable his wife to visit the baths. Early next morning, the man took his pick and shovel and went to work while his wife went to the baths. When she arrived, she found the doors closed. 'What is going on here, why are the baths closed?'—'Because the Chief Rammal's[1] wife is coming.' But the woman begged the attendant to let her in: 'Please let me slip in through the door so that I may sit down in a corner and wash myself. I shall go away very quickly, or keep well out of sight in my corner.' She kept on begging until the attendant allowed her in. Suddenly she saw an ugly and deformed woman approaching, together with two people who supported her arms. This sight disturbed the poor man's wife: she turned her eyes heavenwards and said: 'Oh God, I am so lovely and beautiful and for two months my husband has been unable to scrape together the ten shahi for my bath. There we both are, walking about with rumbling stomachs, while here they lead this crippled, ugly woman with so much fuss, pomp and splendour.' In the end, however, she nevertheless praised God and returned home.

When her husband came back from work in the evening, she told him about her visit to the baths and about the Chief Rammal's wife and said: 'Husband, tomorrow you will go along and also become a Rammal.'—'Leave me in peace, wife,' he said, 'I know nothing about fortune-telling.' But she replied: 'Don't make any excuses. Tomorrow morning you will go and become a Rammal, otherwise I am going to divorce you!'

> If you want to keep me as your wife,
> Better choose a fortune-teller's life!

Tomorrow morning you will sell your pick and shovel and, with the money, you must buy a Raml board and a few old books. Then you will sit down at a street corner and throw your dice on the Raml board.' 'Do leave me alone, woman,' he repeated, 'I don't know anything about this Raml business.' However, all his objections were in vain. 'Don't worry about that,' said his wife, 'I will show you how to go about it. If someone comes along to ask for your advice, all you need to say is: "Oh yes, quite right, your star is under the sign of the scorpion and such-and-such will happen to you." Our merciful Lord will take care of the rest.'

Early next morning the man sold his pick and shovel, bought some Raml equipment, went along to a mosque and sat down. Before long, the groom of the town's richest merchant came to consult him: 'A camel carrying my master's money, and for which I am responsible, has suddenly run away. I do not understand how it could have happened, but the camel is gone. Use your Raml and tell me where the camel is now.' The Rammal thought: 'Lord, giver of all life, what on earth shall I tell him? May my wife's father roast in hell!' Well, he shook his dice and threw them on the board. He thought for a while and then said: 'Pay me one hundred dinar[2]. Then take a few peas and drop them on the ground one by one, follow them to wherever they may have rolled and when you have used them all up, stop, turn around three times and continue in the direction you are facing; walk on, turning neither left nor right, and you will find your camel.' The groom paid the hundred dinar, threw the peas down in front of him and after having dropped the last one he turned round three times and continued walking in the direction he was facing. After walking a short distance, he reached the ruins of a house. And there, believe it or not, the camel lay resting. The groom took the camel's reins, walked back to the house of his master, the rich merchant, and told his story: 'Today such-and-such has happened to me. Then I met a Rammal and he told me certain things, with the aid of his Raml, and so I found the lost camel.'

After the groom had told his master of his experiences and had handed over the camel's load, he returned to the Rammal and gave him ten ashrafi. The Rammal, who the night before had tried in vain to earn even a single shahi, suddenly found himself in possession of ten shining pieces of gold. He was so filled with happiness, he did not know on which leg to stand. As soon as the sun had disappeared behind the mountains, he packed up his belongings and went home. On arriving there, he placed food and drink on the table and said: 'You were quite right, wife, to be a Rammal is not such a bad thing after all.'

Next day, after he had sat down at the same place, a few of the rich merchant's servants and scribes came to him and said: 'Our master wishes to see you.' On hearing this, the Rammal's heart began to pound: 'Oh my goodness, what does he want of me?' He went along, thinking to himself: 'It will be interesting to see the outcome of all this.' And so he came to the house of the rich merchant and greeted him with great respect. The master looked the Rammal up and down and asked him: 'Are you the one who has found the camel that was loaded with my money?'—'Yes, master.'—'From today,' said the master, 'you shall be my Chief Rammal.' With that he again gave him a large sum of money.

In the evening the man returned home and said to his wife: 'The devil knows, woman, you have put me in a very difficult position!'—'What is the matter?' asked his wife. 'Nothing, except that the richest merchant in the town has sent for me and given me all this money and the goods you see here before you, and that he has appointed me his Chief Rammal. So, from today I am the Chief Rammal and yet I know nothing at all about the art. If the master so much as suspects how little I know, truly I could be in great danger.' His wife merely replied: 'The Lord is merciful.'

From that day onwards our Rammal went to the rich merchant's house every morning at daybreak and returned to his home in the evening. For some time nothing special happened. One day, however, it came to pass that forty thieves broke into the rich merchant's treasury. Next morning the merchant called his Chief Rammal and said: 'You must hurry and find the thieves and all the money and valuables they have stolen.' In the evening, on returning home, the Rammal said to his wife: 'Well now you can see, wife, what is going to happen. They will prise open my fists and everybody will see that they are empty. A few thieves have robbed my master's treasury and he has ordered me to catch them and recover the stolen money and valuables. Tomorrow I shall be unmasked before the whole world and disgraced.'—'Dear husband,' said his wife, 'do not lose heart. Tomorrow you must go to your master and ask for forty days' grace. After that we shall see whether you get out of this alive or not.'

Much to his relief, the Chief Rammal was granted the forty days' grace. But on returning home, he said to his wife: 'If I am to lose my life, it will be all your fault. You and I know only too well what no one else knows, which is that I am completely ignorant of the art.' His wife just said: 'The Lord is merciful. Go to the bazaar and buy forty dates. Eat one every evening and throw the stone into the earthen jar over there, so that we shall be able to keep account of the days and know when the fortieth day has arrived.' The Chief Rammal bought forty dates and took them home. In the evening, feeling very worried, he ate one date and threw the stone into the jar, saying: 'That was the first of the forty.'

Now let us hear what happened to the thieves in the meantime. They had heard that the wealthy merchant had a Rammal who was so clever that he knew everything going on in the bowels of the earth as well as high up in the heavens, and he knew exactly what everybody was doing. This was very serious for the thieves and they were beside themselves with worry in case the Chief Rammal caught up with them one day. After all, he had forty days to find the thieves and their loot. They sat round in a circle and put their heads together, trying to find a way out of their predicament. Finally the forty thieves agreed that each evening one of them should creep up to the roof of the Chief Rammal's house and there try to discover what he was doing. So one of them went along on the first evening, just as the Chief Rammal had eaten the date and thrown the stone into a jar, saying: 'That was the first of the forty.' The thief thought the Chief Rammal was referring to him as the first of the forty thieves. He took fright, returned to his comrades and said: 'It is all very well for you to be sitting here quite calmly, but listen to what happened to me! No sooner had I reached the Chief Rammal's roof than I heard him say: "That was the first of the forty!"'

The following evening another robber was sent. When he reached the roof, the Rammal was eating the second date, and as he threw the stone into the jar he called out: 'That was the second of the forty!' Thereupon this robber, too, ran back to the others and said: 'Everything we have heard about this Rammal is perfectly true; No sooner had I climbed on to the roof than he said: "That was the second of the forty."' To cut a long story short, each evening another one of the forty thieves climbed up on to the roof as the Rammal was eating a date. When he threw the stone into a jar, the man on the roof thought the Rammal had called out his number. And when the thirty-ninth evening arrived, they said to one another: 'Even if we were to hide underground or high up in the sky, the Chief Rammal would still find us. It would be far better for us if we confessed our misdeed to him; perhaps he will then show us mercy.' Next morning, the forty thieves, carrying sword and Koran, went to the Chief Rammal's house and swore[3] that they would show him the hiding place of the stolen treasures if only he would allow them to escape unharmed. The Rammal promised to grant their request and they told him that all the stolen goods were buried at a certain place in the desert.

The Rammal went to his master in a happy frame of

mind. As soon as the master saw him approaching, he said: 'Well, Chief Rammal, what have you discovered? Have you found the thieves?'

'May it please you, master,' he replied, 'I have found the treasure in all its splendour. Send camels, horses and mules to a certain place in the desert so that they may be laden with the stolen goods.'—'But where are the thieves?' —'If you please, noble Sir, the robbers have escaped far into the western regions and to catch them would cost twice as much as all the stolen goods are worth.' So camels, horses and mules were sent out. The Rammal went with them and guided them to the place the thieves had described, and all the stolen goods were recovered. The master again rewarded his Chief Rammal with a large sum of money and numerous presents.

On returning home in the evening, the Rammal said to his wife: 'Well, little wife, now I have enough money and treasures to support the next seven generations in a life of plenty, and even then something will always be left over. And now that we have so luckily escaped from that tricky situation, let us consider ways and means of giving up fortune-telling, because otherwise we shall come to a sticky end.' His wife said: 'Listen carefully, husband, tomorrow when your master visits the baths, you must come running along, pushing aside anyone trying to stop you, rush into the baths like a madman, grip the master by the wrist and ankle and drag him out. Then they will all say the Chief Rammal has gone mad and so you will be dismissed.'

In the morning, as the rich merchant was about to enter the baths, the Rammal came hurrying along. The people tried to stop him from entering but he rushed straight into the hot chamber, grabbed the rich merchant by the wrist, dragged him forcibly out of the bath and pushed him into the dressing-room. At that very moment the roof of the hot chamber came crashing down. 'Now you can see,' he said, 'why I came here in such a hurry. I saw on my Raml board that, dear God, the baths would collapse within the next hour and so I rushed here straight away.' The rich merchant, together with all the others present, praised the wisdom and experience of the Chief Rammal most highly. There could be no doubt that the rich merchant owed his life to him. And God only knows how much money and wealth he bestowed upon the Rammal. In particular, he showed him great personal favour and held him in higher regard than anyone else. The Chief Rammal went home again in the evening and said to his wife: 'You can see for yourself, dear wife, it did not work.'—'Yes,' said his wife, 'how can we fight against God's will!' The Chief Rammal continued: 'Try to think of something, wife, because otherwise I will be unmasked in the end.' His wife thought for a while and then said: 'Dear husband, one fine day when all the merchants and nobles of the town are assembled, and your master is sitting on his upholstered chair, you simply take his hand and throw him off his chair. Then the people will say that you are not quite right in the head and will chase you away. Then come back to me and we shall be able to enjoy life in peace.'—'That is a clever idea,' said the husband.

And so, one day when all the merchants and nobles were assembled at the rich merchant's house, the Chief Rammal suddenly rushed in, grabbed his master's hand and pulled him off his chair. Just as he rolled over on the floor, a scorpion as big as a sparrow was seen at the very spot where the merchant's feet had rested a moment ago. The Chief Rammal turned to his master at once and said:

'I was looking at my Raml at home when I saw that a scorpion was about to sting you. This is why I ran here in such a hurry and pulled you away from danger.' This time the Rammal was given even more money than before, and his fame spread throughout the whole world. In the evening he said to his wife: 'Things went wrong again this time.'—'Dear husband,' she replied, 'I am powerless against God's will!'

One day, the rich merchant wanted to go hunting. The Chief Rammal was included in the party and he rode closely behind his master who trusted him more than anyone else. A grasshopper happened to settle on the saddle button of the rich merchant's horse. The master caught the grasshopper and concealed it in his hand. He then turned to the Rammal, saying: 'Now tell me what I have got in my hand.' The Chief Rammal felt as if all reason had vanished from his brain like a puff of smoke. He thought to himself: 'Well, you really have landed among the nettles this time! ... The grasshopper jumped once, the grasshopper jumped twice, now the grasshopper is caught in the palm of the hand.'[4]

At first he spoke those words only quietly to himself, but then he called out loudly: 'The grasshopper jumped once, the grasshopper jumped twice, now the grasshopper is caught in the palm of the hand!' The wealthy merchant thought the Rammal had noticed that he was hiding a grasshopper in his hand. He opened it and the grasshopper flew away.

And so, dear listeners, if it is God's will, even a poor wretch who for two months was unable to earn ten shahi to pay for his wife's bath, can acquire much wealth and splendour. What a man sets out to do, he can achieve with God's help.

7. THE SECRET OF THE BATHS OF BAD'GARD

AT the command of Queen Husn Banu, the Arabian prince Hatim Tai[1] undertook the task of solving the mystery surrounding the baths of Bad'gard. He set out from Shahabad, Husn Banu's city, and after a long journey reached a densely populated city. In front of the city gates stood an old man who greeted Hatim and bade him welcome. Hatim returned his greetings.

The old man said to him: 'It would give me great pleasure to receive you in my house tonight.' Hatim accepted the invitation, so the old man took him to his house and showed him great hospitality. After the meal the old man asked: 'What is your destination, young man, and what is your name?'—'I am from the Yemen,' replied Hatim, 'I have come from Shahabad and am on my way to the baths of Bad'gard.'—'On hearing this, the old man lowered his head and sat in silence for a long time. Then he looked up and said: 'Young man, what enemy has sent you to the baths of Bad'gard? Nobody knows where Bad'gard is. All that I have been able to discover is that not one of those who have gone forth to find the baths of Bad'gard has ever returned. In the city of Qatan there lives a king whose name is Harit. He has posted guards at the frontiers of his realm with orders to bring before him anyone wishing to find the baths of Bad'gard, but nobody knows why he does this, and whether he kills those brought before him or allows them to continue their journey.'

Hatim told the old man that in order to further Prince Munir's courtship of Queen Husn Banu, he had undertaken to perform the seven tasks required by the queen, and that he had already accomplished six of these; the seventh task was to discover the baths of Bad'gard, and it was with this aim in mind that he had once again set forth on his adventures. 'May God be with you and your parents, young man,' the old man resumed, 'because you have risked your own life and have faced many dangers out of love for another. I am sure you are a man of noble birth. But in spite of all this, it would be better for you to return and say that Bad'gard is a cursed place, and that nobody knew anything about it nor where it might be found.'—'How can I possibly return with such an excuse?' said Hatim, 'The unhappy lover is impatiently expecting my return, and the hour is approaching at which I have to fulfil the promise I made.' The old man continued: 'Listen to what I have to say, young man: not one of those who have gone out to find the baths of Bad'gard has ever returned.' 'I know that your warnings are for my own good,' Hatim replied to his high-minded host, 'but if one has accepted a duty before God, one must not turn back half-way; that would be contrary to the commandments of our faith. I trust in God's mercy and hope that through me the young prince will be able to have his wishes fulfilled. Therefore, in God's name, show me the way to Qatan so that I may go there and solve this riddle.'

When the old man realized his guest was determined to proceed with his plan, he accepted the inevitable and showed Hatim the way out of the town. After walking a considerable distance, the old man said: 'From here onwards you must keep to the right. After you have passed through several towns and innumerable villages, you will see in front of you a mountain with many cypresses growing at its foot. You must cross the mountain; you will then reach a wide plain, beyond which you will come to a place where the path divides. There you must follow the path to the left because although the right-hand one is less arduous, it is fraught with danger and horrors.'

Hatim took his leave of the old man and started his journey. He passed through towns and villages and observed the busy life of the people, and after some time he reached a town. On approaching, he heard drums beating and trumpets sounding. 'They must be celebrating something very special here today,' he thought, and as he entered the town he saw that a large number of people had gathered. Beautiful tents had been erected beyond the gates of the town; around the tents carpets were spread out, and here the people sat together while dancers and singers entertained them. Pots had been placed over the fire and food was being prepared in them.

Hatim approached and asked the reason for these joyous festivities. 'The position is this,' they replied: 'Every year a mighty dragon comes from the desert out there and assumes human form. Then all the young girls of the town, from the king's daughter to the beggar's daughter, are brought out to these tents, dressed in bridal gowns and adorned with golden trinkets, then a great feast is celebrated. The dragon carefully looks at all the young girls and takes away with him the one he likes best. The only reason why we arrange all these joyous festivities is that we are forced to. God alone knows which girl the dragon will choose today and force to marry him. The following day, however, everyone mourns and wails, and sorrow and sadness reign in the town for a whole week. Today is the day the dragon is expected.'—'This means,' said Hatim, 'that the gay feast is in truth an occasion of mourning for you.'—'Yes,' they replied, 'but what can we do to put an end to our terrible calamity? Who might be able to rid us of this dragon?' On hearing this, Hatim said: 'As a service to God I shall avert the tragedy from your heads tonight and you may therefore be of good cheer.'

When the people heard these words, they went to the dignitaries of the realm and told them what Hatim had said. Hatim was taken before the king; he was invited to be seated on the throne by the king's side and told: 'Young man, do you know anything of the evil that plagues us?'—'Yes,' replied Hatim, 'this dragon is of the race of the Djinns, and as they are of a wicked nature he has strayed from the path of righteousness and made himself a tormentor of human beings.'—'If he really is a Djinn,' said the king, 'and it is within your power to rid us of this calamity, you would be doing us the greatest kindness imaginable.' Hatim, on his part, said to the people: 'Now you must carefully obey my instructions. When the dragon has selected one of your daughters you must say to him: a young nobleman has arrived and ordered us not to allow the young girl to depart without his consent. While you, in your anger, may be able to destroy our country within one year, he is capable of turning it into a desert instantly.'

They promised to do exactly as he told them. As the day drew towards its close and the dragon's arrival was imminent, the people came to Hatim and reported that the monster was approaching. Hatim told the king that he intended to go out and take a close look at the monster, and the king and the Emirs went out of the palace as well. At that moment Hatim saw the dragon approaching: he was so tall that his head reached far into the sky and his length defied all description. Stones and bushes were ground to dust under his feet. 'Only God is almighty!' Hatim thought at that moment. As the dragon approached, he beat so mightily with his tail that the people were made breathless and they all threw themselves on the ground face-downwards. The dragon looked around in all directions, then he lay down and assumed the appearance of a handsome man. The king invited him to the castle and allowed him to sit on the throne. After they had partaken of some food, the dragon rose and said: 'Now let me see your girls.'—'You need only to look and choose,' said the king.

The dragon left the castle and walked about looking at the daughters of all the chieftains and merchants, as well as at the other young girls, but none really pleased him. He then returned to the open square outside the castle, entered the royal tent and demanded to see the king's daughter. She was brought along. The Djinn at once fell in love with her pretty face and said: 'I love this one, I want her for my bride.' The king, however, said: 'The son of one of my dignitaries, who has been far away from this city for a long time, has now returned and I dare not act against his orders because if I disobey him, he could destroy my realm within an hour. If it pleases you, I will send a messenger to him and then I shall have to act as he decides.'—'Let him come,' said the Djinn.

Hatim was sent for and he stood facing the Djinn, who said: 'Young man, I have not seen you in this town before. Where are you from and why are you misleading the people? Do you want me to destroy this country?' Hatim replied: 'Before I came here everybody submitted to your will, but now I am heir to this city and anything concerning it must be approved by me. In my homeland certain traditional ceremonies have been observed since time immemorial. The intended bridegroom must submit to these ceremonies before the bride is placed in his care.'—'What are these ceremonies?' asked the Djinn. 'The first is this,' replied Hatim: 'I have here a charm which I inherited from my ancestors; this is to be placed in a beaker of water and the future husband must drink some of it.'—'Just give me the water,' said the Djinn, 'and I will drink it.' Hatim produced a charm which had been given to him[2] by the daughter of the bear, and dipped it into a beaker of water which he handed to the Djinn who, without suspecting anything untoward, drank it, thereby losing his magic powers.

Hatim continued: 'The second ceremony requires the bridegroom to climb into a large vat[3] which is then sealed carefully, and whence he must try to escape. If you succeed, you shall receive the bride; if not, you will have to give me one thousand rubies and two thousand precious diamonds of the kind found in the land of the fairies before you can be given the bride.' The Djinn, relying on his supernatural powers, said: 'Just bring the vat!' Hatim gave orders for a large vat to be brought and invited the Djinn to jump in. This he did, following which Hatim sealed the opening of the vat, blew over it and pronounced the name of the Almighty. This caused the cover to become as hard as rock. 'Now try and come out again!' Hatim called to the Djinn. However, try as he might, the Djinn was unable to escape. Hatim then ordered a large quantity of wood to be piled up. The people hurried away to gather the wood, which they placed around and above the vat. Then they lit the wood. When the Djinn began to feel the heat inside the vat, he cried for help, but none was forthcoming and he had to die a miserable death. Hatim then gave orders for the vat to be buried deep in the ground and said to the people: 'Rejoice, because the evil that has plagued you for so long will never trouble you again.'

Everybody from the richest to the poorest and the king, as well, blessed Hatim, and he was presented with a huge amount of gold; but he said: 'Dear friends, I do not need your gold, what I have done was for the glory of God.'—'It is only a modest gift,' said the people, 'and we are deeply indebted to you for the great service you have rendered us.' Thereupon Hatim asked that the town's poor and needy be called together and he distributed the gold among them, and they offered prayers, asking God to bestow his blessings on Hatim.

Hatim stayed a further three days, then he took leave and continued his journey. After a short while he reached the mountain of which the old man had spoken. After crossing the mountain he walked on and saw a vast plain ahead of him. He traversed it for several days and many of God's miracles and signs were revealed before his eyes. Sometimes he was able to drink fresh water from a spring, on other occasions he had to quench his thirst with brackish water.

He left the plain behind him, and on reaching the point where the road divided he thought of nothing except that the old man had told him the road to the left was full of danger, and 'honour your elders and take heed of their advice'. He therefore took the road leading to the right. After walking for only a short time, he suddenly remembered the old man's words very clearly and realized that he had taken the wrong road. 'I had better turn back and continue along the road to the left,' he thought to himself, and he turned back to look for it. However, he was caught among thorny shrubs, which tore his flesh, causing him great pain and suffering. 'The old man was right when he said this road was full of terror,' thought Hatim, 'and I am sure that after these thorns I shall have to endure other troubles.'[4]

After travelling for several days and suffering a thousand tribulations, he finally emerged from the bushes and entered the desert. 'There were innumerable wild beasts in the desert and as soon as they saw a human approaching, they rushed at him. Hatim saw that the monsters advanced in their thousands. They resembled a cross between foxes, jackals and panthers. Hatim was terribly frightened. 'They will eat me,' he thought, but he did not know how to defend himself against them. So he stood there, shaking with fright and not knowing what to do. Suddenly the old man appeared at his right-hand side and said: 'Young man, it is always advisable to heed the words of older and more experienced men. He who rejects their advice will find himself in peril, and that is what has happened to you. 'Honoured sir,' Hatim replied, 'I know that I was foolish not to follow your advice.' 'Well, then,' the old man continued, 'throw down the charm given to you by the bear's daughter and see what God's power can achieve.'

Hatim quickly produced the charm and threw it on the ground, while the old man disappeared before his eyes. The ground first turned yellow, then black, then changed to green and finally it became red. As soon as the red colour appeared, the beasts went completely berserk, attacking and tearing each other to pieces. Hatim was amazed at this sudden ferocity among the animals. They had abandoned their intention of attacking him and had started devouring each other instead. When he saw that not one of them remained alive, he offered a prayer of thanks to God and picked up his charm.

After travelling for several days, Hatim reached a forest of ore. No sooner had he entered the forest, than he felt the ore splinters pierce his shoes. He tore strips from his clothes and stuffed them into the shoes, but this did not help and soon his feet were cut and sore. Finally he managed to reach the edge of the forest. He sat down and took off his shoes. The soles of his feet were perforated like a sieve. Hatim extracted the ore splinters, bandaged his feet with rags and put on his shoes again. He limped on, glad to have survived all these tribulations. But while he was crossing the plain, scores of giant scorpions, scenting human flesh, rushed towards him. They were as big as jackals, had birds' claws and their eyes flashed like those of wolves. In this hour of peril, the old man once again appeared by the side of the shaking Hatim and reminded him, as before, to use the charm. Once again the earth assumed different colours and as soon as it had turned red, the scorpions attacked each other and fought amongst themselves with such ferocity that none survived.

After Hatim had travelled for a long, long time, he finally reached the city of Qatan and put up at a hostelry. There he rested for a few days. He then took two magnificent pearls, two rubies and two splendid diamonds, put them in his pocket and went to the king's palace. The guards and chamberlain reported his arrival to King Harit, who ordered them to find out more about the young traveller. The chamberlain returned and asked Hatim: 'Where are you from and who are you?'—'I am a merchant,' replied Hatim, 'and I am on my way from Shahabad. I respectfully request permission to appear before the king.' The chamberlain took this information back to the king, who ordered the stranger to be brought before him at once.

When Hatim stood before the king in the hall of the royal palace, he spoke the customary phrases and, praising the king, he spread out his jewels as a present. On seeing the jewels, the ruler's face lit up; he allowed Hatim to sit beside him on the throne and asked him: 'Young man, where is your caravan?' Hatim replied: 'I gave up being a merchant a long time ago so that I could lead the free life of a wanderer, because this world is but an empty shell and it is unwise to devote one's heart to gold. When my road took me to the frontiers of your realm and I heard the king being praised so highly by everybody, I decided to pay my respects to the monarch who is so just and treats his subjects with such kindness.'

The king gave him a splendid suit of clothes and showed him great friendliness, saying: 'Young man, stay here for a few days and give us the pleasure of your company.' Hatim accepted. The king allowed him to reside near the palace and Hatim remained at the royal court for six months. He made himself so indispensable to King Harit that if one day the king did not see him, he immediately sent a messenger for Hatim and was not at ease until he arrived. The king frequently said to his courtiers: 'It would please me greatly if this young man were to settle down in our city for good.'

One day, when Hatim found King Harit in a particularly happy mood, he produced a few beautiful gems, rubies and emeralds, and handed them to the king. 'Young man,' said Harit, 'your generosity and nobility of mind please me greatly. You have paid respects to me for such a long time and never expressed a single wish. Therefore, speak freely and tell me whatever may be on your mind; I will grant you any wish, because I should like to do something for you.' Hatim replied: 'As long as the king is happy, I wish for nothing else. Travellers do not need much.' However, when Harit urged him, he said: 'May the king enjoy a long life. Well, there is but a single wish in my heart and as long as it remains unfulfilled it will pursue me to my last hour.'—'And what is this wish of yours?' asked Harit. 'Even if you wanted to marry my own daughter, I would give her to you.'—'May your daughter be a mother and sister to me,' replied Hatim, 'but my wish concerns something quite different. If the king will promise to grant it, I shall name my wish.' Harit replied: 'I will grant your wish'; and he swore a solemn oath by his sacred faith. Thereupon Hatim said: 'It is my wish to visit the baths of Bad'gard. With your permission I will go there and explore them.'

When the king heard these words, he lowered his head and remained seated in silence for a long time. 'Oh king,' Hatim said finally, 'why are you so quiet?' Harit looked up and replied: 'Young man, many are the thoughts that passed through my mind. The first is that having made a solemn promise never to permit anyone to travel to Bad'gard, I would be breaking my word if I gave permission now. The second thought is that none who have gone there have ever returned and that it would be a great pity if I were to lose you—such a handsome, noble young man—for ever; because, my thoughts ran on, I would never have anyone like you at my court again. Finally I reflected that by refusing your wish, I would be breaking the promise I gave you in advance, and in that case no one in the whole world would ever be able to rely on my word.' —'Oh king,' replied Hatim, 'if it is God's will I shall return safe and sound and shall again pay my respects to you;

do not worry about this.' And then he explained to the king why he had set out to solve the mystery surrounding the baths of Bad'gard, and he finally told him his name. Harit rose, embraced Hatim and said: 'Yes, your brow is indeed noble, the splendour of your generosity is known throughout town and country, and within a short time your name has become a shining example to all the world.' He then gave orders for a pass to be issued which Hatim was to present to Saman Idrak, the guard of the baths of Bad'gard. In addition, the king ordered a few men to accompany Hatim and then he rose from his throne, embraced the prince once again and said farewell. After Hatim had gone, the king left the throne room, and with tears in his eyes withdrew to his private suite in the palace.

Hatim left the town and continued his journey, exchanging cheerful conversation with his companions. After riding for fifteen days without a break, they at last saw a gate. Hatim asked: 'What is that over there, looking like the dome-shaped summit of a mountain?' His companions replied: 'That is the gate to the baths of Bad'gard. We are still one week's journey away and shall have to ride for another seven days and nights.'

They rode on and arrived at the gate after one week. It was then that Hatim saw a vast army lined up and he asked: 'What is the meaning of this army?' His companions told him: 'Saman Idrak, the keeper of Bad'gard, has moved into the field with a huge and powerful army. He allows nobody to go near the baths without producing a written order signed by the King of Qatan.'

Hatim went to meet the soldiers. They knew his companions from Qatan well, and had many friends among them. They greeted each other and the men from Qatan said: 'Here is a young man from the Yemen who carries a pass signed by King Harit, and the king has ordered us to accompany him.' Hatim handed the pass to Saman Idrak. He opened it and read: 'You are required to grant this young prince from the Yemen access to the baths because I have given him my word of honour. However, if it is at all in your power to make him see reason and persuade him to return, you may be sure of a generous reward.'

After he had read these words, Saman Idrak showed Hatim the greatest respect, allowed him to take his seat at the place of honour and treated him most hospitably. In this manner he managed to keep Hatim at the house for several days and gave him good advice and important instructions. Hatim, however, asked his host not to try and dissuade him. When Saman Idrak realized that Hatim was not to be swayed, he wrote to the king: 'This young man, the bearer of your pass, will not be dissuaded and refuses to listen to our advice. What are the king's orders now? Am I to admit him to Bad'gard or not?' In the meantime, Hatim tried daily to persuade Saman to conduct him to his journey's goal while Saman, for his part, postponed the visit from one day to the next until the arrival of the king's instructions granting Hatim permission to visit Bad'gard. Thereupon Saman said to Hatim: 'Young man, are you tired of living, since you will not listen to what I am telling you? There is still time for you to return and save your life; otherwise, you are doomed and will regret your obstinacy too late.' Hatim, however, asked Saman to forgive him for insisting on his intentions.

Saman, who saw quite clearly that nothing would dissuade Hatim, then conducted him to the baths. Hatim looked at the gigantic gates which reached far into the clouds. Never in his whole life had he seen such a high gate before. The front of the gate bore the following inscription in Syrian: 'This haunted place was built during the reign of King Gayomard and will continue to exist as a symbol for a long time to come.[5] Whoever falls under the magic spell will never escape alive. Bewilderment and horror will be his lot. He will suffer hunger and thirst and, though he will be able to eat from the fruit of the garden and see all that is to be seen there, he will have great difficulty in ever leaving this place alive.'

After Hatim had read these words, he thought to himself: 'This inscription on the gates does in fact reveal to me the mystery of the baths of Bad'gard. Why then should I go in?' He was about to turn back when it occurred to him that he had not yet found the true answer to the riddle of the baths. 'What must be done, shall be done,' he said, 'I have to go in.' So he took leave of his companions, walked a few paces and entered the gate.

On looking back to discover whether his companions were following or had remained outside, he could see neither the men nor the gate, but only an endless desert as far as the eye could reach. At that moment Hatim really grasped the meaning of the name of Bad'gard;[6] he understood that anyone who places his foot beyond the gate is faced with his own destruction, and said to himself: 'Oh Hatim, you will lay your bones to rest in this desert.'

He looked around in all directions but could see nothing except the same wilderness. And so, chancing his luck, he simply started walking. He walked for many days and after having covered a considerable distance, he saw a human figure coming towards him. On approaching, Hatim saw that it was a young man carrying a mirror under his arm. He greeted Hatim and handed him the mirror. Hatim took it and, looking at the reflection of his own face, said: 'May one use these baths, and are you the barber?'[7] 'Yes,' replied the man. Hatim continued: 'Where are the baths?' 'The baths are farther along the road,' the man replied. 'Are they the baths know as Bad'gard?' 'The very same.' When Hatim heard this, he was pleased and continued his questioning: 'Why have you left the baths?' 'It is part of my duties,' replied the barber, 'to come out and meet any strangers who arrive here, to conduct them to the baths and attend upon them, and then I receive a gratuity in return. If it pleases you, follow me to the baths and I hope that a little of your wealth will come my way.' 'Very well,' replied Hatim, 'I have just completed a long journey and should like to bathe today.'

The barber led the way. They walked for about a mile until they saw in front of them a dome which appeared to reach well into the sky. Hatim asked what this building was. 'These are the baths of Bad'gard,' the barber told him. When they reached the building, the barber entered and invited Hatim to do likewise. He complied but as he turned round to close the door behind him, he saw that it was already sealed by brickwork. 'You will probably never be able to leave these baths again,' he thought. In the meantime the barber had shown him as far as the pool and said to him: 'You may enter the water now and I will bring you some hot water.'—'But I cannot enter the water fully clothed,' objected Hatim, 'I must have a loin cloth.' The barber brought him a clean loin cloth. Hatim undressed, sat down at the edge of the pool and wrapped the cloth round himself. Then he went into the pool. The barber handed him a bowl of hot water which he poured over his head. The barber returned twice with a full bowl but as Hatim poured the water over his head for the third time, a terrible noise was heard and the whole of the baths was shrouded in darkness. For some time Hatim stood in the dark, confused, but gradually light returned and the barber and the pool had vanished; only the dome remained, towering like the inside of a rocky cave, and the entire space was filled with water which reached half-way up Hatim's calves.

Hatim was very frightened and asked himself what the meaning of all this witchcraft might be. Meanwhile the water continued to rise. Now it reached as far as his knees. Hatim waded about, looking for an exit. He searched everywhere but was unable to find a door or any other way out. Soon the water had risen as far as his belt. Once again he looked around everywhere in despair but could find no escape. By now, the water had risen as far as his neck. Hatim, who was able to swim, managed to keep his head above water, but all the time he thought: 'This is probably why none of the men who entered here have ever returned. They must have drowned here and you, too, Hatim, will perish in these floods. There is no escape. After all, King Harit in Qatan did his utmost to keep me away from here. Very well then, when man comes face to face with death, he should turn his eyes to the merciful God. Oh Lord, I have placed all my power into the service of good—I have only one life, but even if I had a thousand lives I would devote them all to you. Thy will be done!'

Hatim tried to console himself with such thoughts, while the waters kept rising until Hatim's head touched the highest point of the dome spanning the centre of the baths. Exhausted by swimming, Hatim extended his hands to hold on to the inside of the dome and rest a little. At the same moment, however, a mighty thunder was heard again and he suddenly found himself standing outside in the desert where nothing but endless desolation could be seen. 'If I have escaped from the floods,' he thought, 'I should be able to escape alive from all this sorcery, too.'

He walked for three days and nights and then he noticed a tall building. Hoping to find some inhabitants there, he approached the building and saw that it was surrounded by a huge garden. The garden gate was open, Hatim passed through, but suddenly the garden vanished before his eyes and as he turned round to go out again, there was no trace to be seen of the gate. 'What kind of fresh torment is this?' he thought. 'Have I still not escaped from this sorcery?' In the meantime the garden had appeared again and as Hatim was forced to remain in it, he walked about under the fruit-laden trees and saw a large variety of flowers which opened their petals and shone in numerous colours. Hatim was hungry and so he took and ate many of the fruits growing in the garden, but no matter how much he ate he remained just as hungry as before. He consumed almost a thousand pounds of fruit, but his hunger remained unsatisfied. However, he took fresh courage and continued his journey in a more confident mood. As he reached the castle, he saw a large number of stone statues standing around in the forecourt. Surprised, Hatim asked himself what the meaning of these statues might be, but there was nobody present who could help him unravel the mystery.

While Hatim was standing there, deep in thought, he heard a parrot from within the castle: 'Young man, why do you remain standing there? How did you get here and why have you decided to end your life?' Hatim looked up and listened to the voice. Suddenly, he noticed this inscription above the entrance to the castle:

'Oh servant of God, you are unlikely ever to leave the baths of Bad'gard alive. This place is under the magic spell of Gayomard. One day, when Gayomard was out hunting, he found a diamond which sparkled like the blazing sun and the shining moon. He picked it up. It was extremely heavy, weighing more than three hundred mitqal.[8] Greatly surprised, he asked his courtiers and sages whether there existed another diamond like it. They replied: "From the day the heavens were created no one has ever seen such a large and shining diamond." Thereupon Gayomard said: "I shall keep it in a place where no human being will ever be able to reach it." And so he created this magic work as protection for the diamond, and built the baths of Bad'gard. The parrot in its cage is also part of the magic. Oh servant of God, inside the castle you will find bow and arrows on a golden chair. If you have any wish to escape from here, you must take the bow and arrows and shoot the parrot. If you hit it you will have broken the spell, if you miss you will be turned into a stone statue.'

After reading these words, Hatim regarded the stone figures and said plaintively: 'So this is how these statues were created and you, too, Hatim, will end your days in this witch's cauldron where men are robbed of their senses. However, man proposes and God disposes.'

With these thoughts in his mind he entered the castle, took the bow and arrows from the golden chair, placed an arrow against the bowstring and aimed at the parrot. The bird flew up to the ceiling and the arrow missed its target. Hatim's legs turned to stone up to his knees.

The parrot returned to its former perch. 'You had better be on your way, young man,' it mocked, 'this is no place for you.' Hatim, holding the bow and arrows in his hand, jumped—but had to stop a hundred paces away from the bird. His feet were too heavy for him to move any farther or even to lift them from the ground. His eyes filled with tears as he said to himself: 'What a terrible thought—having to live here for days in this terrible and pitiful condition! Better shoot again, Hatim, so that you may become like these statues.'

He shot the second arrow and missed again. Thereupon the lower half of his body turned to stone. The parrot had again flown up towards the ceiling and, while flying back to its perch, said as before: 'You had better be on your way, young man, this is no place for you.' Hatim, with bow and arrow in his hand, jumped—but again had to stop a hundred paces away from the bird. He cried and said: 'May nobody fail to hit his life's target like me!' There was only one arrow left. He placed it in the bow, commended his soul to God and aimed at the parrot. 'God is great!' he called and closed his eyes as the arrow left the bowstring. And contrary to all expectations, the arrow struck the bird, which dropped out of its cage. A huge cloud of dust arose, thunder rolled and the earth was shrouded in darkness. Confused by all this noise, Hatim thought he was about to be turned into a statue. However, as the thunder receded and Hatim opened his eyes again, he noticed that garden and cage, golden chair and bow and arrows had disappeared, and in their place an enormous diamond lay on the ground shining like the blazing sun. Hatim bent down and picked it up. His legs were no longer of stone and all the statues had been turned into living people again. When they saw Hatim, they asked: 'Young man, how is it that you are still alive? Where is the garden?'

Hatim told them exactly what had happened. Thereupon they all came up to him, threw themselves at his feet and swore to serve him as slaves. Hatim ordered them to follow him to Qatan, but nobody knew in what direction that city was to be found. However, fortune smiled upon them and they succeeded in finding their way, and after walking for several days they saw the tall gate through which they had entered the baths of Bad'gard. Beyond the gate they found Saman Idrak, the guardian of the baths. Hatim greeted him and told of his adventures. Saman Idrak entertained Hatim and his companions in his house and then allowed them to continue their journey. After several days' travel Hatim reached Qatan where he went to see King Harit. The king received him with great honours, allowed him to sit down by his side and asked Hatim to tell him about his experiences. Hatim gave the king a detailed account and then he produced the diamond, placing it before the king with the following words: 'I have brought this diamond with me to show you, but I must take it to Queen Husn Banu.' Then he added: 'Give these men, who have accompanied me here, a horse each and some money for the journey and let them return, each to his own country.' This was done and Hatim and King Harit took leave of the men. Then Hatim also asked for permission to continue his journey. Harit gave him a large retinue, Hatim set out, and returned to Shahabad after a long journey.

Husn Banu's people recognized Hatim and took him to the queen's palace. She received him in her private suite, listened to his story and looked at the diamond which he took from a pouch and placed before him. 'Now it is for you to honour your pledge,' Hatim said. The queen kept her promise and the wedding of Queen Husn Banu and Prince Munir was celebrated. After the festivities, Hatim returned to his home in the Yemen where his home-coming caused great rejoicing. His father handed over his crown and realm as Hatim's inheritance, and Hatim spent the rest of his life in happiness and pleasure.

8. MUHAMMAD THE MASTER MARKSMAN

THERE lived a woman who had a son, a tall, gangling lout; he was called Muhammad, the master marksman. He was a real idler and good-for-nothing and his poor mother had to be up and about from early morning till late at night, taking in washing for people and going begging, just to provide food and clothes for him. He had inherited the name 'Master Marksman', together with a broken bow and a few arrows, from his late grandfather.

One day, when the old woman had gone out to work for their daily bread, Muhammad rose from his bed and searched all over the house until he found one qran[1] in a box belonging to his mother. This was money the poor old woman had put aside for cases of dire need and the boy took it. He used those hundred dinars to buy some date syrup which he took home with him. Lazy as he was, he soon fell asleep. When he woke up, he saw thousands of flies gathered round the syrup pot. He tried to hit them with his hand and squashed a few of them, while the others flew away. That, he thought, was a deed of great bravery. He therefore rose, took his broken bow and went to a teacher who was sitting in the street holding class. 'Mr Teacher,' he said, 'take these ten shahi and write the following words on this bow in clear and bold letters:

> "Many thousands he defeated and slew in battle,
> Many thousands fled to escape from him."'

The teacher inscribed these words on the bow and handed it back to Muhammad.

Since he had killed the flies, Muhammad considered himself a mighty warrior. He took his bow on his back and left the town, intending to move elsewhere and to proclaim himself a warrior although, in fact, he was so weak that if anyone as much as pushed him he would tumble head over heels and fall flat on his nose. Nevertheless, he set forth. After wandering for a few days he stopped at a house and went in. There were all sorts of weapons in the house but nobody was in sight. However, a delicious smell of food lured him into the kitchen. There was a pot on the fire containing food enough for over one hundred people. 'This house,' he thought, 'must be inhabited either by the Divs or the Peris. No matter who might be living here, I am terribly hungry and tired. I shall take some of this food and lie down. I do not care what happens afterwards.' No sooner said than done; he hung up the bow somewhere above his head and fell asleep.

There was a city two miles away from this place. The king who ruled there had forty warriors and they used this house as their quarters. During the day they went out to enjoy the pleasures of the hunt and at night they returned to their house. On this day, the warriors returned from the hunt some time during the afternoon and they saw a tall youth lying there comfortably, fast asleep. Above his head there hung a bow on which was written:

'Many thousands he defeated and slew in battle,
Many thousands fled to escape from him.'

The warriors thought they had before them a soldier who had accomplished all those heroic deeds and, being famous in his own city, he was now travelling to other places. They consulted amongst themselves and said: 'The best thing to do would be to show him friendship and if he wishes, we shall present him to the king, so that he may be allowed to live here with us.' On awakening, Muhammad saw that he was surrounded by forty strong men. He was so frightened that his bile turned to water and he was unable to utter a single word. The warriors took his silence as a sign of pride and fearlessness and addressed him with great courtesy: 'Brother, we welcome you here since you have bestowed upon us the honour of your visit. Please regard us as your brethren. We are warriors like yourself and we hope you will enjoy our company.' When Muhammad heard these friendly words, he was slightly encouraged. It occurred to him that the inscription on his bow must have had this effect and so he started to talk freely and to brag about how he won this and that battle and how he had killed several wild lions. After they had talked at length, they ate their evening meal together and lay down to sleep.

Next day they said to Muhammad: 'Come, let us go hunting together.' He replied: 'I am still tired after my journey and would rather rest a little while you go hunting. Meanwhile, huntsmen's greetings to you!'

In the meantime, the king had become involved in a war. He gave orders for the warriors to assemble and he sent out a horseman to fetch them. The horseman arrived and found a stranger in their house. 'Where are the warriors?' he asked. 'The Sultan has become involved in a war and has ordered me to call the warriors.'—'They went out hunting,' replied Muhammad, 'they will probably return at sunset.' The horseman tethered his horse and sat down to wait. While sitting there, he discovered Muhammad's bow and, having read the inscription, he thought to himself: 'This is just the man we need to defeat the king's enemies.' They soon started talking and Muhammad again began to brag, without realizing that by doing so he only created difficulties for himself.

When the warriors returned from the hunt, the rider gave them the king's message. They all lowered their heads as a token of obedience and promised to start the following morning. Then they introduced Muhammad to the horseman and said: 'He is a great warrior, the like of whom the world has never seen before. When he appears on the battlefield, the enemy will scatter at once.' The poor wretch listened to these words of praise and did not know what to say. He nodded his head unintentionally and they all believed the coming battle was just the right thing for him. Muhammad, however, thought: 'How stupidly I have behaved. The wretched inscription I had affixed to my bow will now prove to be my undoing. Having led the life I did, how should I be able to mount a horse tomorrow?'

During that night Muhammad was unable to sleep a wink. Next morning, when the time had come to start, a powerful and fiery horse was brought before him. Surprisingly enough, he managed to talk himself out of that situation, too. He said to the others: 'If I am to shoot with my bow, I shall have to use both my hands and then I could easily lose control over my horse in the heat of battle. It would therefore be better if you took a linen belt and strapped me to the horse.' The warriors were somewhat surprised at these words but they thought this was part of the higher art of warfare such as was customary in his country. And so they tied him to the horse with a linen strap and then they all rode out to the battlefield. Muhammad, unable to control his horse, drifted first to one side and then to the other in the turmoil and confusion of the cavalry engagement. Finally, he made straight for the enemy camp. Everyone admired the audacity with which he threw himself, single-handed, into the very heart of the enemy army. The horse, with Muhammad on its back, raced along and he nearly fainted with fright; finally they galloped past a tree. Muhammad, shaking with fear, threw his arms round the tree and held on to it with such strength that he tore it from the ground together with its roots and he rode on, without releasing the tree. When the enemy soldiers saw a horseman with a whole tree in his arms riding towards them, they fled in panic and the others won the battle.

The king himself witnessed Muhammad's bravery. He called Muhammad before him, praised him highly and presented him with a robe of honour. He then gave orders for Muhammad to be moved into quarters at the royal castle. Muhammad, however, thought quietly: 'How fortunate that the tree, together with its roots, came away by itself, because I am not even strong enough to uproot the smallest bush from the ground.'

After some time had passed, the vizier came to the king and said: 'The city guard has reported that the lion is on his way to fetch the prey to which he is entitled according to our agreement.' This greatly saddened the king. He did not know which of his unfortunate subjects he was to take and throw before the lion. The situation was this: in the woods not far from the city there lived a lion which attacked all the animals and people he could catch, causing great alarm and despondency among the people. For that reason an agreement was made with the lion, according to which he was to stop his attacks and in return he would be given a sheep every day and a fourteen-year-old girl once a year. This treaty had been in force for many years, and no one had dared so far to kill the lion.

After the king had thought about this matter a little,

he sent a messenger to Muhammad. He appeared and the king explained the position to him, saying: 'If you kill the lion, you shall become my son-in-law.' Muhammad, who shook with fright whenever he saw so much as a horse, was beside himself when he heard the word 'lion'. What was he to reply to the king? He thought of one thing and another and finally he said: 'Very well, let me see where the lion performs his evil deeds.' He felt sure there would be an opportunity for him to run away. The people led him to the woods and called out: 'There is the lion!' And with that, they ran away. Muhammad stopped. The lion, smelling a human being, let out a terrible roar. Muhammad ran away, horrified, and climbed up a nearby tree. The lion roared again and settled down below the tree. When Muhammad saw the terrible animal exactly underneath, his limbs began shaking and he was no longer able to hold on. He fell out of the tree and landed squarely on the lion's back. And as he sat astride the beast, he involuntarily pulled the lion's ears and steered him towards the city. The king was standing there with his courtiers and was awaiting the outcome of the fight, when suddenly they saw Muhammad riding along on top of the lion. The assembled crowd was jubilant. The king ordered his executioners to cut off the lion's head; when that had been done, he gave his daughter to Muhammad in marriage and they celebrated their wedding in pure joy.

9. SA'D AND SA'ID

ONCE upon a time there lived a woodcutter. He went out into the steppe every morning to gather a load of brushwood which he sold in the city. With the money thus earned he maintained himself and his family. One day, after he had wandered across the steppe as usual, he collected so much brushwood that he was unable to carry it all at once. He therefore put it down in a cave, intending to collect it the following day. It so happened, however, that there was so much rain and snow the next few days that he was unable to go out and collect the brushwood. During that spell of bad weather, a caravan happened to pass by the cave. The travellers needed the wood for lighting their camp fire, and then they moved on.

When the weather improved and the ground had dried, the woodcutter left his house and went into the country as usual. He found that his brushwood had been burnt but on looking more closely, he discovered that the roof of the cave consisted of pure gold. He took some of the gold and hurried home with it. He sold the gold and with the money had a beautiful house built for him to live in. He then collected the remainder of the gold and as a result of his patience and piety he soon became a wealthy man.

Some time later, God gave him two sons. One he called Sa'd and the other Sa'id. When the boys reached the age of twelve he sent them to school. Then he bought them a chicken with which they played every day. A short time later the chicken laid two eggs, but these eggs were like precious stones and shone in the night. The woodcutter took the eggs to the bazaar and there he sold them to a Jew for one thousand toman. The Jew asked him: 'Have you any more eggs like these?'—'If the chicken lays some,' replied the woodcutter, 'I shall have more.' The Jew consulted a book and discovered that the chicken must be a lucky one and that he who ate the head of the chicken would become King, and he who ate its liver would find one hundred toman under his head every morning.[1] He thought hard, trying to find a way of gaining possession of the chicken.

At that moment an old woman happened to pass by. The Jew called her and said: 'Listen, mother, do have a look round in the town tomorrow and see whether you can discover a chicken of such and such appearance and if you have found it, come back here and let me know.' The old woman promised to carry out his instructions. The very next morning she went into the city and searched and probed until she reached the woodcutter's house. She poked her nose in and discovered the chicken the Jew had described to her. She struck up a conversation with the woodcutter's wife and soon made friends with her. Then she went back to the Jew and told him she had found the chicken at that particular house. 'Very good,' said the Jew, if you can prevail upon the mistress of the house to obey me, I shall give you anything you ask for.' The old woman went back to the woodcutter's house and started talking to his wife, trying to persuade her. At that moment the woodcutter entered the house and went past them. Thereupon the old woman said to his wife: 'My daughter, is it not a pity that you have spent your life in misery in the company of this man?'—'Dear old mother,' replied the woodcutter's wife, 'nothing can be done about that.'—'If you are willing to enter into an agreement with me,' the old woman continued, 'I shall introduce you to a young man who will give you joy for the rest of your life.'

After the old woman had thus made an agreement with the woodcutter's wife, she took the good news back to the Jew. He gave her a handful of gold coins and then she fetched the woodcutter's wife and introduced her to the Jew. When the young woman came to enjoy his love, he said to her: 'Kill your chicken and prepare a dish from it for me and then I will give you my love. I shall come and visit you this afternoon.'

While the Jew was at the baths, the woman returned home, killed the chicken and cooked it.

In the meantime the two boys came home from school. Their mother was not there when they arrived and so they sat down and ate from the dish that had been prepared. As chance would have it, one ate the chicken's head and the other its liver.

Shortly afterwards the Jew arrived. The woman was standing outside in the street, waiting for him. She showed him into the house and asked him to sit down while she went into the other room to fetch the food. When she noticed that the boys had eaten from it, she beat them; thereupon they ran away and hid. The mother, however, placed the remainder of the food before the Jew. He noticed immediately that the chicken had neither head nor liver. 'May God have mercy upon you, woman,' he called, 'this seems to me a strange manner of offering hospitality to one's guests by serving half-eaten dishes!'—'You must forgive me,' she replied, 'but my sons have just come home from school and have eaten from the food without dreaming who it was really intended for.'—'I want the chicken's head and liver,' the Jew said, 'and besides, I have eaten at least a hundred chickens of this kind and more than a hundred women would be glad of the opportunity of enjoying my love.'—'What am I to do?' asked the woman. The Jew knew right away how to handle the situation. 'If you want to become my lover,' he said, 'you must cut open your sons' abdomens and take out the chicken's head and liver so that I can eat them. Once that has been done, I shall submit to your wishes. I will give the boys some medicine to make them well again.' Thereupon the woman agreed to do as he demanded.

Now let us hear how fate tricked the Jew. While he was talking to the woman, Sa'id was standing behind the wall and listened. He went up to Sa'd and said: 'Dear brother, come and let us run away. Mother has fallen in love with this Jew and is planning to kill us.' Then he told Sa'd everything he had heard and that very same evening they both fled to the desert. When the woman called her sons, they were not to be found anywhere and soon loud wailing was heard from the woodcutter's house. When the woman saw what misfortune she had brought upon her head, she began crying and lamenting. 'I have behaved disgracefully,' she cried, 'now I cannot embrace my Jew and I have lost my dear children.'

In the meantime the two boys wandered farther out into the desert. When night fell, they lay down, put their arms around each other and slept. They rose at dawn. Then Sa'id discovered a bag filled with pieces of gold where his head had been resting. He picked up the bag and gave it to his brother, asking him to look after it. They walked without stopping until they reached a spring about noon. Here they rested for an hour and then Sa'id got up and walked about a little. He discovered a board with the following inscription: 'Know ye, oh human children, that if two people walk on from here together, they will both perish. Therefore they should each go their separate ways. He who chooses the path to the left will be reunited with his beloved after many tribulations, and he who takes the path to the right shall be given a king's honours.' Sa'id and Sa'd embraced each other and cried for a long time. Then they walked on, each in his own direction, Sa'd going to the right and Sa'id to the left.

After Sa'd had walked for four days, he reached a city. He went to the bazaar where many horses and large quantities of arms were on sale. He bought a suitable set of weapons and continued on his way from one city to the next on horseback. Finally, he reached a city whose inhabitants had just assembled outside the gates. Sa'd asked what had happened, and was told that the king of this city had died and that the law provided in such a case for a falcon to be released. The man upon whose head the falcon settled would be proclaimed king, even if he were a stranger or a beggar.

Sa'd spurred his horse to speed to the place and to see whether the falcon might perhaps land on his head. The soldiers had already released the falcon twice and each time he had fluttered about a little and settled on a wall. The soldiers were much surprised at that, but when they saw a horseman approaching from the distance, they waited a short while until Sa'd came closer. Then they let the falcon fly once again and this time he made straight for Sa'd and settled on his head. Some of the people refused to accept this sign and demanded a repeat of the trial, but once again the falcon landed on Sa'd's head. Thereupon he was raised upon a shield and borne into the city with the appropriate honours where he was dressed in regal robes and placed on the throne. From the very outset he endeavoured to conduct the affairs of state in a just manner and although he was the child of poor people, he knew how to conduct himself like a nobleman.

And now let us hear how Sa'id fared. He moved from one place to the next and every morning he found one hundred toman under his head. This is how he became a wealthy man within a short space of time. He nevertheless continued travelling from one city to another until he reached the city of Haleb. Here he walked about for a time and finally came to a castle. In front of the walls sat a few wretched men, covered in sackcloth and ashes. He went up to them, engaged them in conversation and asked whose castle this was. They replied: 'The mistress of this castle is a Chinese woman by the name of Dilaram, and as far as we are concerned, we came here, each from his own city, and spent everything we possessed because this woman Dilaram demands one hundred toman for every night one spends in her company.' Sa'id thought: 'This will suit me well! I get my hundred toman every night anyway.' And so he entered the castle.

Dilaram had forty slave girls who looked so much like herself that no one could tell the difference. She sent one of her slave girls every night to sleep in the arms of her lover in Dilaram's stead. In this manner Sa'id spent forty nights of delight and joy. Dilaram, however, knew exactly what happened during those forty nights and so she found out that Sa'id put his hand under his head every morning and produced a bag of money to pay his debts. She also knew that Sa'id had eaten the liver of the lucky chicken, and decided to take the liver from him because it could never be digested. And so she sent for him. Very old wine was served and she gave him large portions. When he lay there, drunk and unconscious, she hit him on the back with such force that the chicken liver flew out of his mouth. She then fried and ate the liver.

When Sa'id woke up next morning, he looked under his head in vain—there was nothing there. He was unable to remember what had happened and he only thought: 'There is no money today and I must therefore go and obtain some.' With tears in his eyes he left the castle and wandered out into the desert where he walked on and on until he became so tired he had to sit down by the wayside.

A short while later three horsemen came riding along. They asked Sa'id where he had come from and where he was going to and he replied: 'I was employed by the Kadi of the city but I have fallen out with him and now I am on my way to another country.'—'Listen to us, please,' the three horsemen said to him, 'we are having a dispute. We are brothers. Our father has died and we distributed his whole legacy with the exception of three items.'—'Who was your father?' asked Sa'id. 'He was a Jew called Simeon,' they replied. 'Very well,' Sa'id continued, 'what are you going to pay me if I settle your dispute?'—'Each of us will give you three pieces of gold.' Sa'id said: 'Show me the three things.' They produced the three things, which were a small leather bag, a small carpet and a jar of eye ointment. 'Each of you can take his own item,' Sa'id remarked, but they replied: 'Young man, each of these things has some very special properties. If one sits down on the carpet and says: "In the name of King Solomon, take me to such and such a place," the carpet will at once rise up into the air and fly along and land at the desired place. The special feature of the bag is that any kind of fruit or other food one may desire can be taken from it. But he who spreads some of this ointment over his eyes, becomes invisible to all.'

Sa'id settled the dispute as follows: 'I am going to place three arrows against my bowstring and will shoot them off. The one of you who brings one of these arrows back to me first, shall be owner of the three things.' He placed three arrows against his bow and shot them off in different directions. The horsemen immediately rushed off in pursuit of the arrows but as soon as they were out of sight, Sa'id prayed to God for protection, sat on the carpet and flew away. When the horsemen returned, they saw the carpet high up in the air and they beat their foreheads and called out: 'Oh why did we reveal to him the mysterious properties of these things!'—Sa'id, however, called down to them from the air: 'Why are you beating your foreheads in despair at the fact that divine justice has prevailed? Your father once schemed to have me killed, but God did not want me to die then.'

With these words Sa'id flew away to Dilaram's city where he descended at a lonely spot. He at once took out the jar of eye ointment, coated his eyes with its contents and, having thus made himself invisible, entered Dilaram's castle. She was just sitting down to a meal. When he saw her, Sa'id was so overcome by emotion that he fainted, but he soon recovered and started to partake of her food. To her horror she had to watch the food disappear from one side of her plate, without understanding what was happening; and when he also took water from her cup and she heard the gulping sounds, she was so frightened that she fainted. Sa'id went away without having been seen by anyone.

At daybreak Sa'id took a magnificent apple from his bag and went with it to Dilaram's castle. As the result of a rumour according to which the mistress of the castle had fallen ill, a large crowd had gathered in front of the gate but Sa'id pushed them aside and went up to the head of Dilaram's bed. When she finally recovered from her fainting fit, she saw him standing there. Sa'id handed her the apple and said: 'I have undertaken a journey to the Garden of Iram[2] and have brought you this medicine.' After she had eaten the apple, he said: 'Our account for last night has not yet been settled; come with me to my quarters and receive your money.' Dilaram stood up and followed Sa'id to his hostelry. There he once again took some fruit from his bag and offered it to her. Later on, he sat down with her on the carpet and flew away with her.[3] Dilaram wailed and cried: 'Where are you taking me?'—'Keep quiet,' he replied, 'we are flying to your castle.' And then he abducted her to an Island near the Indian coast.

After the carpet carrying them had descended, Sa'id wanted to enjoy Dilaram's love, but she rejected him. 'But I did, after all, spend forty nights sleeping by your side,' he said.—'No,' she replied, 'I have forty slave girls who look exactly like me and each night I sent one of them in my place.'—'But this time there will be no substitutes,' said Sa'id. When Dilaram realized that she had no hope of escaping, she said: 'I shall not submit to you unless you promise to marry me.'—'That is precisely my wish and you shall be my bride,' replied Sa'id. In this manner he overcame her resistance.

They spent forty days and nights on the island. Dilaram, however, tricked Sa'id; she flattered him and stroked him and turned his head to such an extent that finally he revealed to her the magic properties of the wonderful things. One day Sa'id undressed to take a bath. Dilaram made use of this opportunity, took the jar of ointment, the bag and the carpet and Sa'id's clothes as well, sat on the carpet and said: 'Take me to my castle!' The carpet at once rose high up into the air and took her to her castle.

When Sa'id came out of the water and saw that his companion had disappeared, he beat his face with despair. For three days and nights he wandered about aimlessly on the island, uttering heart-rending cries of woe. Finally, he settled down under a tree, surrendered his heart to grief and, completely immersed in painful thoughts, he fainted. Suddenly three doves came flying along and settled on the tree. One of them said to the other: 'Dear sisters, do you know that young man down there?'—'No,' they replied. The other one continued: 'It is Sa'id. He loved Dilaram but she refused to have anything to do with him. In his love for her, Sa'id has told her all his secrets and she has shamefully deserted him and left him behind on this island, lonely and in despair. But one day he will obtain satisfaction.'—'Sister,' said one of the other doves, 'what is there for him to do?' The first one spoke again: 'I am going to tell, just in case he is awake; he may hear my words and that may perhaps enable him to reach the goal of his wishes. If he cuts a small piece of bark from this tree and wraps it round his feet, he will be able to walk across the sea. If a leaf from this tree is placed upon the eyes of a blind person, he will see again and if a madman is allowed to smell the fruit of this tree, his sanity will be restored. But if a donkey is beaten with a twig from this tree, he will be turned into a human being, and if a human is beaten with it, he will be turned into a donkey.' After the dove had thus spoken, all three flew away.

In the meantime, Sa'id had recovered from his fainting fit and had heard everything. He followed the dove's instructions, tied some of the bark from the tree round his feet and jumped on the water, and after crossing the sea he reached the coast without mishap. Then he travelled farther through the country from one hostelry to the next until he reached a city where the king's daughter was suffering from an attack of insanity and where the king had publicly declared that he who could restore her reason would have her as his wife.

Sa'id went up to the king and said: 'Give me your daughter in marriage if I can restore her reason and if I should fail, you may kill me.' The king agreed. The princess was brought along. Sa'id allowed her to smell the medicine and she began sneezing at once and the madness left her. 'Who are you?' she asked. 'How did you, a stranger, manage to enter my chamber?' Sa'id replied: 'I am your husband.' The king was informed of what had happened and he ordered that the good news be conveyed to the people by the beating of drums. The wedding feast lasted seven days and nights, and this is how Sa'id found his bride.

A few days after the wedding Sa'id went up to the king and said: 'Grant me permission to travel because I have an enemy upon whom I must wreak vengeance.' The king asked: 'How big an army do you need?'—'I do not need an army,' Sa'id replied, 'all I need is a black slave.'

The king thereupon allowed Sa'id to go forth and he travelled to Dilaram's city where he stayed in a caravan-serai. After dark he took his twig and went to Dilaram's castle. The servants and guards tried to bar his way but Sa'id extended his twig and they were all turned into donkeys. Then he went to Dilaram's chamber. When she recognized him she became extremely angry, and said: 'You fool, who gave you permission to come in here?' She called for her servants: 'Arrest this uncouth lout and put him in chains!' When nobody responded to her calls, she rose to see what had happened. There were no slaves nor slave girls to be seen, but only a large number of donkeys. Before Dilaram was able to recover from her surprise, Sa'id beat her with his twig and turned her into a donkey, too. He sat upon the donkey and rode out from the castle to his own quarters and there he told a servant: 'Put a bag on this donkey's back, sweep up all the dirt in this hostelry and put it into the bag, take it out and throw it into that pit over there.' The servant did as he was told and continued working until darkness fell. He then put a little hay and barley before the donkey. Dilaram, however, who was a pampered young woman, wept bitterly at her humiliation.

To be brief, three days passed in this manner. Sa'id's heart burnt with pity for her and finally he went up to her, saying: 'How do you feel in your present state? If you give me back the jar of eye ointment, the bag and the carpet, I shall release you.' With these words, he struck Dilaram with his twig and restored her to human shape. Then he gave her some clothes to put on. She approached him lovingly and handed over everything in her possession. Afterwards wine was served and Dilaram drank some of it and regurgitated the chicken's liver.

Sa'id then took Dilaram with him and journeyed to the country where he had married the king's daughter. Later he sent a messenger to his parents, who had both lost their eyesight in the meantime. Sa'id said to his mother: 'What you have done has turned out for the best.' And after he had told her everything that had happened to him he took out the leaf from the wonderful tree and placed it on his father's and mother's eyes and their sight was restored at once. The mother deeply regretted what she had done. In the meantime Sa'id had sent a messenger to his brother Sa'd, who accepted the invitation and they celebrated their reunion in joy and happiness.

A short time later the father of the princess died and Sa'id inherited his realm and so he, too, gained a throne after many calamities.

10. THE THREE COMRADES

THERE once lived three men who decided to team up and go somewhere to earn their living by trickery. One of them had a sparse beard, the second was bald and the third was an opium addict. When they arrived in Ispahan, they drew lots to decide which of them was to test his skills first. The bald man lost and so he had to go out and try his luck that day and see what spoils he could bring home.

So the bald man left the room which they all shared. He stopped outside an eating house and considered his situation. He did not have a penny in his pocket, and said to himself: 'I will go in here and fill my belly. At worst, I may get beaten up.' He therefore went straight in, called the cook's servant and ordered several dishes, thinking to himself all the time: 'They will tan my back in any case, but it does not matter—by that time I shall have eaten my fill.' He rolled up his sleeves, sat down comfortably and started eating. After he had finished, the cook came and demanded payment for the food consumed. The bald man looked around in all directions and spotted a money box containing a gold piece. 'Now you listen to me,' he said, 'have I not just given you a gold coin? Hurry up and give me my change! Or were you perhaps trying to cheat me?' The cook realized at once that this could develop into an unpleasant situation. So he took the fellow by the collar with one hand, gripped his throat with the other, pushed him against a wall and kept beating the bald man against it until he started bleeding. When the bald man saw blood, he called the cook all the names under the sun and yelled: 'Help, help! Robbers, murderers!'

It so happened that the town's police chief was passing. When he saw what was going on, he asked: 'What is the meaning of all this? What is going on here? The bald man pushed forward and shouted: 'Sir, I have taken a meal here and paid with a gold coin, but when I asked for my change the owner beat me and made my head bleed. The gold coin is still in the cash box over there.' The police chief immediately took hold of the cook, gave him a resounding slap on the face and said to him: 'You son of a whore! You take gold coins from the people and then you beat them up as well!' He then turned to the bald man and said: 'You need not pay anything for what you have eaten. You may consider your bill settled by the beatings you received. Here is the gold coin, take it and be off.' The bald man grabbed the gold coin and disappeared. On returning to his comrades he threw the gold coin down on the floor and said: 'Look, you scoundrels, here is my loot for today! Tomorrow it will be your turn and then we will see what kinds of pranks you can think up.'

Next day it was the opium addict's turn. He also was ready to go out and try some roguery. He awoke early in the morning. 'Oh God,' he thought to himself, 'if only I could think up something good so that my comrades will not scold me!' Throwing his coat over his shoulder, he went out. He roamed the streets until he met a woman, who called to him: 'I say, man, are you a stranger here?'—'Yes, little sister,' he replied, 'I am a stranger and completely on my own.' The woman continued: 'Will you accompany me to the Kadi and help to get me a divorce?[1] You shall then receive ten toman for your trouble!'—'Little sister,' he said, 'I will do exactly as you ask. In God's name, therefore, lead the way and I will follow.' And so he accompanied the woman to the Kadi, in order to receive his money.

On reaching the judge's chambers they saw the thick-bearded, black-turbaned Kadi sitting there, busily reading a book. The opium addict greeted him and said: 'Dear Kadi, this woman here is my wife. I don't want to keep her any longer; please be good enough to read the divorce formalities for me.'

'Dear friend,' said the Kadi, 'why do you wish to be divorced from your wife?' He replied: 'I no longer care for her. She roams the streets without my permission, and a woman who spends her time outside the house without her husband's permission is no good.'—The Kadi saw that nothing could be done here, and he pronounced the divorce.

After the divorce procedure was over, the woman took the man aside. She was hiding a small child beneath her cloak. She took the child out and said: 'Just hold this child until I come back with your money.' The opium addict took the child into his arms and walked it into the street. There he stopped and waited for the woman. When she failed to return and collect the child, he went back to the Kadi and said to him: 'Dear Kadi, where is the wife from whom you have just divorced me?'—'You had better stop this, friend,' said the Kadi. 'I have given you your divorce, but how in God's name can you expect me to know your wife's whereabouts? You must know where she is usually to be found. Just keep on looking and you will find her.'

There the opium addict stood with the child in his arms. He was hungry—and the child was hungry. He walked along the streets and occasionally spoke gently to the child:

'Who might your father be?' he asked sometimes, and at others he said: 'Where could your mother have gone after she burdened me with you?' Finally he thought: 'I will simply put the child down in a corner and disappear.' With these intentions he entered a derelict mosque. As chance would have it, only the day before, a woman had abandoned a small child in that mosque and disappeared without being noticed, and for this reason the caretaker of the mosque was on his guard. Suddenly he saw a man approach slowly and carefully, unwrap a small child from his coat, put the child down and walk hurriedly away. The caretaker ran after him and called: 'Stop, you scoundrel! Where do you get all these orphans which you bring here before running away?' With these words he grabbed the opium addict, beat him thoroughly, placed the two children—the one left the previous day and the other brought by the opium addict—into his arms, struck him a few more times across the neck, and said: 'Now be off, you good-for-nothing, and never let anyone see you here again!'

Once more the opium addict walked the streets. Now he had a child in each arm. 'You cursed brats!' he grumbled. 'Why did you have to cross my path today of all days and bring misfortune on my head?' When he passed by some derelict baths, he put both the children down in a corner and escaped. However, a man standing at the corner of the baths noticed him and shouted: 'Son of a bitch! Bastard! Where did you get these little children you are throwing down?' The opium addict kept running, pursued by the man. They both ran as fast as they could. Suddenly the opium addict noticed an open door and rushed in, head over heels, in order to hide. Inside he saw a staircase, and in his mortal fright he raced up the stairs and sat down on the centre step. 'Oh God,' he thought, 'they'll soon catch me and push both children into my arms again.' Suddenly there was a knock on the door. 'Oh God,' he murmured, 'here they are! I do not know which mousehole to crawl into, or where to escape.' Meanwhile he saw a slave girl coming along and opening the door. Outside stood a well-dressed young man who said to her: 'Go in and tell your mistress that the man has arrived who spent some time with her at a certain place, and who has an appointment with her.' The girl took this message to her mistress, and the woman said: 'Ask him to go upstairs, I shall follow soon.' The girl returned to the young man and told him: 'My mistress will appear soon, be kind enough to go into the upstairs room.'

When the opium addict saw the young man mounting the stairs, he hurriedly hid in a back room. A few minutes later a heavily bejewelled lady appeared and followed the young man upstairs. They disappeared into a room together, where they embraced and kissed. The lady soon became more amorous and the young man's ardour grew. The opium addict sat right behind the door and observed everything.

In the midst of all these happenings, the lady's husband appeared. The girl, who was posted as a lookout to warn her mistress should anybody be coming, ran up the stairs, calling: 'Dear lady, there is going to be trouble now, the master is here!' The woman sprang to her feet. 'My love,' she said, 'go into that back room and hide.' The opium addict heard this and quickly hid in one of the two earthen grain jars standing in the background. A moment later the woman's lover came in and slipped into the other grain container.

The husband entered. 'Well, wife,' he said, 'what are you doing up here?'—'I'm sweeping and cleaning,' she replied, 'and it really is necessary for me to do so, because this girl does not do her job properly.'—'Oh my dear master,' the slave girl began, 'you have no idea how much work your wife takes upon herself and how hard she finds it.' To which the master replied: 'I have brought a few bags of flour with me, empty them into that container over there.'—'Better not,' said his wife, 'because that one has a crack and there is also a dead mouse in it. You had better pour into the other one.' She knew of course that her lover was hiding in the first one. The woman and the girl then took the bags of flour, dragged them to the second storage vessel and emptied them into it. The opium addict pinched his nostrils, closed his mouth and trod the flour under him. As fast as the women poured it in, he pushed it under him. Suddenly the grain jar broke into two pieces and the unlucky opium addict was revealed, covered all over in white flour and sitting in the midst of it. At first, they were all frightened because they thought he was an evil spirit. But then the husband called: 'Fool, how did you get in there? And what are you doing here?'—'I came with my master,' the rogue replied. 'And what kind of a dog is your master?'—'He is sitting in the container over there,' said the opium addict. Now it was the wife's turn to gape. The husband took an axe and struck the grain jar, and at that moment the other ass of a man appeared and crawled out. 'You there,' said the husband, 'where do you come from?' The lover began: 'I lost my way and entered this house to see whether anybody could direct me. But you followed right behind me and I took fright and hid here.' The husband and the lover went for each other and started to fight;

whilst this was going on, the opium addict took the opportunity to absent himself. Outside, in front of the house, he shook off the flour, saying: 'Dear God in heaven, that was a strange way to give me my daily bread!'

As he walked along the street, a smell of sweet cakes came to his nostrils. He was plagued by hunger and thought to himself: 'I will enter this house. And even if they beat me up I shall not mind in the least, the main thing is to get some bread to eat.' And so he entered the house. There a young man and a woman sat side by side. They kissed and embraced, while the woman had to mind the bread in the oven at the same time. 'Listen, you ass,' the lover said to the opium addict, 'what do you mean by entering somebody else's house like this? Get out of here or I will break your head!' In the meantime the husband entered. 'Well, well,' he said, 'this is charming! Haven't I heard often enough that my wife is a hussy? I did not want to believe it at first, but now I can see it with my own eyes. You filthy slut! For whom are you baking these cakes? It is quite plain that you are keeping lovers.' The woman replied: 'I'm baking only for those two unfortunate strangers who have lost their way and have no relatives here.'

During all this time the opium addict did not let the cakes out of his sight for a moment. 'Sir,' he addressed the husband, 'you have a wife who is exceptionally noble and kind. May you be spared the sorrow of ever losing her.' With these words he started to collect the cakes. The woman made secret signs to him: 'Where are you going with these cakes?' The opium addict also answered with signs: 'Just be quiet, I will keep them until your husband has gone.' He filled his arms with cakes and withdrew cautiously until he reached the door, and disappeared.

A short while later he appeared before his comrades and said: 'Look, you scoundrels—and what trouble I have had to obtain these cakes! But tomorrow it's the sparse-beard's turn.'—'Very well,' said the sparse-beard, 'I'm going to sleep here tonight and tomorrow I will tell you what prank I shall perform.'

Next morning the sparse-beard arose and said to his comrades: 'Take me to the Takht-i-Fulad quarter of the town, put me into a coffin and cover my face with a piece of cloth. Then you must sit down, one by my head and the other by my feet, cover your face with your hands and wail: "Oh poor father, oh unhappy father!" All passers-by will feel obliged to give you something.' His companions did as he told them and after a comparatively short time they had collected quite a nice sum.

As luck would have it, a State official happened to be walking past. He carefully observed the goings-on and noted how the dead body in the coffin counted the money and how he kept saying: 'You sons of dogs! How much money have we taken so far?' The official thought to himself: 'Well, well, you scoundrel! I would be unworthy of being called a man if I failed to bury you alive.' Then he went up to the men and said: 'I have been ordered by the government to wash, dress and bury with my own hands any stranger who dies here.' And, turning to his own men he said: 'Take the coffin on your backs, boys.' The bald man and the opium addict begged and beseeched him, saying: 'Sir, we have been able to collect a little money and will gladly bury him ourselves. So save yourself the trouble.' The official, however, ignored them completely and had the coffin brought to a morgue; then he sent his men away. He put the body on a board normally used when washing corpses. While washing him he kicked him in the ribs several times, saying: 'You bastard, what kind of a corpse is it that counts the money which has been collected?' But the sparse-beard suffered all the blows and kicks and lay quite still, not uttering a word.

Meanwhile, the bald man and the opium addict had reached the morgue and started shouting: 'Sir, what are you doing with our dead man? We wanted so much to dress the body ourselves and arrange for the funeral.' The official turned round to shut the door in their faces. When the sparse-beard saw that the official was turning his back on him, he quickly stretched out his hand and reached into a dish filled with halva[2] standing near the coffin, took a handful, put it into his mouth and gulped it down. The official noticed immediately that the dead man had eaten some of the halva. 'Just wait,' he said, 'you infernal scoundrel, I shall give you something that will do you good.' He then took the man and plunged him into a basin in the morgue, holding him under water for a while. The sparse-beard took this opportunity to quench his thirst with a few gulps of water, but otherwise kept perfectly still like a real corpse. By that time the official had begun to find the whole business less amusing. He dealt the sparse-beard a few blows with his fist and kicked him in the ribs, saying: 'You son of a filthy slut! What a strange corpse you are! You have eaten halva and drunk from this stinking water.'

Meanwhile it had become dark. The official, who had sent his men away, did not know what to do. Suddenly he heard whispering behind the wall. He strained his ears and heard somebody say: 'Let us go into the morgue, it is quiet there and we can share out our loot undisturbed.' There was no doubt that it was a gang of thieves who had robbed a caravan and stolen the valuables. The official feared for his life and therefore decided to lie down in the coffin next to the sparse-beard. The robbers entered. They saw the two bodies lying there, pushed them aside and sat down. Among the stolen objects there was a sword. One of the thieves said: 'The sword belongs to me.' Another countered: 'He who succeeds in slashing this corpse in two with the sword shall have it.' At that moment a third man rose, rolled up his sleeves and said: 'This is just the thing for me. I am going to cut the two bodies in half with a single blow.' The official whispered to the sparse-beard lying next to him in the coffin: 'Comrade, are you going to lie here and let them kill us? Can't you think of anything?' Suddenly the sparse-beard rose from his board, clapped his hands and called out: 'Arise, you dead, and take hold of the living!' The official immediately jumped from the coffin and shouted: 'Grab them and strangle them!'

When the robbers saw that the dead were rising, they ran away as fast as they could, abandoning their loot. But afterwards they said to one another: 'The dead will not take our booty. One of us must go back and see what is going on.' One of them stepped forward and said: 'I am prepared to go and see whether or not the dead have gone away.' The sparse-beard, however, was on guard. As soon as he saw one of the robbers approaching, he hid behind the door. When the robber put his hand round the door to see whether the dead were still there, the sparse-beard grabbed his cap and called to one of the dead bodies: 'Here, this can be your share, it's worth seven pennies.' On hearing this, the robber took to his heels and returned to his comrades. 'Friends,' he said, 'they have so many dead bodies in that morgue that each was given a share of only seven pennies from our booty. There was even one who had not yet received any of his share and so they took my cap instead.' Thereupon all the thieves crept away.

Next morning the sparse-beard said to the official: 'Come, let us be friends and divide the loot.' And then the sparse-beard took his share, returned to his colleagues and told them all that had happened.

Farewell, many thanks, this is the end of my story!

11. THE VALUABLE BIRDS

A MAN went into a bird-seller's shop to sell his parrot. 'How much do you want for your parrot?' asked the bird-seller. 'One hundred toman,' replied the man. 'What!' the shopkeeper exclaimed, 'how can you demand one hundred toman for such a small bird?' 'Because it is a particularly clever bird,' replied the parrot's owner, 'it can talk.' The bird-seller nevertheless refused to buy the parrot, saying that the price was much too high.

During the conversation, the parrot's owner noticed a turkey in the shop. 'How much do you want for this turkey?' he asked. 'One hundred toman.' 'Are you seriously demanding one hundred toman for it?' the man asked. 'Why not? Your bird may be able to talk, but mine can think!'

12. THE DOG'S LAST WILL

THERE was a man who owned a dog which guarded his house faithfully and honestly for many years. The dog grew old and finally died. The man placed it in a coffin, which he took to the Mohammedan burial ground and buried. Thereupon several people went to the Kadi to complain about the man having buried his dog in the consecrated ground of the faithful. The Kadi summoned the man and said to him angrily: 'Why have you committed such a shameful deed? I shall have to sentence you to death.' 'May it please your honour,' said the man, 'to grant me permission to explain the whole matter. After I have told the full story you may act as you see fit. This dog has lived in my house for many years and served me day and night. In return he received his fixed wages every month. I gave him thirty pounds of bread, six pounds of butter, fifty eggs and twenty-four pounds of meat. Before he died, the dog made his last will and said: "All the wages I have received in the past shall go to the Kadi."' Upon hearing this, the Kadi drew out his handkerchief, started to cry and said: 'May God have mercy upon his soul! ... What else did he say in his last will?'

13. THE DEAF MAN

A DEAF man went to visit a sick friend, and thought: 'Although I may not be able to hear, I bet two to one that if I ask the patient how he is, he will answer: "Very well, God be praised!" If I then ask him the name of his physician, he will mention a certain name. And if I finally ask him what medicine he has taken today, he will tell me that he has taken such-and-such a mixture.'

So he entered the sickroom and asked: 'How are you?' 'Very poorly, indeed,' replied the patient, 'I think I am at death's door.' 'God be praised!' said the deaf man, and continued his questions: 'Who is your physician?' 'The angel of death,' replied the sick man. 'Oh yes, he is a very skilful physician and bestows blessings upon all whom he visits. What medicine have you taken today?' 'Poison and venom!' 'May it do you good!' said the deaf man, 'that is exactly the right treatment for you and you could not wish for anything better!'

14. THE PHYSICIAN AND HIS SON

A PHYSICIAN was in the habit of taking his son along with him when visiting the sick. One day he set out, accompanied by his son, to attend one of his patients. He felt the man's pulse and said: 'The patient has eaten pomegranates.' 'Yes, that is quite true,' said the relatives, 'we gave him some yesterday.' 'And he has also eaten some curdled milk,' the physician continued. 'Yes, he had some of that as well.'

On the way home, the son asked his father how he knew that the patient had been eating curdled milk and pomegranates. 'Nothing could be simpler,' said the physician, 'I saw a few pomegranate peels in a corner and I noticed traces of curdled milk in the man's moustache. I know that when there is a sick person in the house, and the others eat, they usually give some of the food to the patient.'

Next day the physician's son went to visit the sick. He felt the patient's pulse and said: 'The patient has eaten donkey meat.' 'No,' said the people, 'he certainly has not.' The young man went home to his father and told him what had happened. His father asked: 'What gave you the idea that the patient had been eating donkey meat?' 'Well, when I entered I saw a donkey saddle lying on the floor but no donkey, and I was sure that the people in the house had eaten the donkey and given some of it to the patient.'

15. THE SURETY

A MERCHANT had to go away on business and he therefore told his apprentice: 'You must not give credit to any customer.' While the merchant was away a swindler came and bought goods worth one thousand toman, saying: 'I will pay for everything tomorrow.' The apprentice said: 'But I do not know you. Therefore, take this ring belonging to my master and put it on your finger so that I may recognize you next time I see you.' The ring was very valuable; the customer put the ring on his finger and the apprentice never saw him again.

16. THE THREE SCHOOLMASTERS

A HORSEMAN was riding along when he met three akhunds,[1] who had just been earning their living by teaching children. He bade them 'good morning' and rode on. 'He greeted me,' said all three and as they were unable to agree among themselves to which of the three the horseman had said 'good morning', they started quarrelling and finally decided to ask the horseman himself. And so they ran after him, calling him until he stopped his horse. When they had reached him, they asked: 'To which of us did you say "good morning"?' He replied: 'To the biggest fool among you.' So each one of the three teachers wanted to be the biggest fool. The best way of finding out, they agreed, would be for each of them to relate one of his follies so that they could decide and agree which of them was the biggest fool.

The first one began his story: 'One day, when I was sitting in school, surrounded by my pupils, who were just doing their work, it so happened that a chicken fell into the well. I tied a rope round my body and lowered myself into the well while the children were holding the other end of the rope. When I was about halfway down the well, one of the children had to sneeze but the others failed to clap their hands.[2] This made me angry and, still hanging in the well, I called out: "Why do you not clap your hands?" The children immediately let go of the rope and clapped their hands and I fell to the bottom of the well, breaking a leg so that I have been limping ever since. Can anyone imagine a greater folly?'

'That is nothing,' said the second one, 'but listen to me now: one Saturday I restarted school. The children, who had been free the previous day,[3] had arranged among themselves that tomorrow one after the other would say to the teacher that he was looking ill. The first pupil entered, said "good morning" and sat down, saying: "Please, sir, what is wrong with you? You look so pale. I am sure you must be sick." Then the second pupil entered and said: "Why is it, sir, that you are looking so hollow-eyed?" And the third pupil said: "Your nose has become very peaky. What are you suffering from?" This convinced me that I was really ill. I gave the children the rest of the day off, went home and told my wife to fetch the doctor. She went and as I was beginning to feel very hungry in the meantime, I rose, went to the pantry and opened the door. There, I found a few rice and meat balls left over from the day before. I began to eat and had just put one rice and meat ball into my mouth when the doctor entered before I had time to get it down. There I stood, with the meat ball in my mouth, unable to swallow. The doctor examined me and thought my face was swollen. "We shall have to lance this," he said and before I knew what was happening, he produced his scalpel and cut open my cheek. On withdrawing the scalpel he noticed a grain of rice at its tip. "This is a small worm," he said to my wife, "can you see how skilfully I extracted it? Had I not done so, your husband would have been dead by now." The doctor collected his fee and I had to stay in bed for several days until the wound had healed while the children were having a holiday and were playing to their hearts' content. I cannot imagine any other folly comparable to mine.'

'That was a mere trifle,' said the third teacher. 'I believe that I am the biggest fool. Listen to me: one morning I went out to the pond to wash myself. When I noticed my reflection in the water, I believed it to be a thief who was hiding in the pond and I called the children. They came running along and I gave each of them a stick and told them: "There is a thief hiding in the pond. I shall now enter the water. All of you will now take up your positions and if you see someone coming out of the water, it will be the thief and you must all beat him with your sticks.' And so I went into the pond and dived but search as I might, I was unable to find anyone else down there. At long last I had to raise my head above water, but the children, believing that what they saw was the thief, started beating me about my head and face with their sticks, forcing me to put my head under water again. This went on for some time. I stayed under water as long as I could but each time my head appeared above the surface, the children started beating me. I called to them, telling them I was their teacher and not the thief, but it made no difference. At long last my wife came and rescued me.'

The horseman gazed at the three teachers and then said: 'My greetings were addressed to all three of you.'

17. THE LAND OF HAPPINESS

In the city of Audjin[1] there lived a merchant named Aziz. His cup of life was filled with the wine of happiness, and the bowl of his existence overflowed with the nectar of wealth. He richly enjoyed his earthly power and possessed a fortune in worldly goods. The bed-chamber of his hopes glowed in the candle-light of fulfilled wishes, and his life was scented with the spice of happiness. His heart, like the source of sunlight, was free from the dust of earthly sufferings and the mirror of his soul was like the shining face of the moon, free from all stains of peevish fate. The heavens had spread out before him the carpet of wellbeing in the house of joy. There was no glory on the sandalwood-scented face of the earth which did not grace the table of his fulfilled wishes, and the emerald[2] vault of the heavens did not contain a single constellation that failed to bow to his will. For him time passed with the sound of lute music and the clinking of glasses, while he stretched on the cushions of pleasure with the bride of his desires resting against his breast. The scented flowers of his soul gained freshness in the gardens of merriment, and the zephyr of happiness made the rosebuds of his heart smile under the gentle breeze on the meadows of paradise.

> He lacked neither singer nor cup-bearer nor wine,
> Until late at night gentle sleep embraced him,
> The web of his life was spun only by joy,
> No human being could live more magnificently.

One day he had again spread the carpet of happiness; he gave a joyous banquet rich in pleasure and merry company, and together with his friends he drank, out of crystal-clear goblets, pure wine from the grape glowing in the evening sun. Intoxicated with joy, he felt as if the heavens' blue dome and the sun's golden cup were filled to the brim with the wine of his wishes.

Just as the gentle spring of gaiety had reached its peak, a stranger appeared on the horizon of his fate. The stranger took his seat on a corner of the carpet and while doing so, he cast an eye veiled with sadness over the assembled group, and from the jewel boxes of his eyes delicate tears fell on his cheeks like pearls. On hearing the stranger's cold sigh, the merry guests suddenly felt as if their mirror of joy had been clouded with the rust of worry, and a cry of anguish pierced the souls of the table companions. Aziz, too, lost the reins of self-control and began questioning the stranger. However, no matter how insistent his questions became, the stranger only remained silent, not allowing a single sound to escape from his lips. Such behaviour only increased Aziz's surprise and plunged him into the whirlpool of impatience. Driven by curiosity, he gripped the young man's coat and plagued him to reveal his soul's secret which had caused the sudden collapse of the company's gaiety. When the young stranger saw that Aziz's desire to learn the precious secret exceeded all bounds, he reluctantly decided to speak, and said:

'Although the matter about which you question me is not something that is offered for sale on earth, and is a jewel that cannot be found in the mine of speech; although I know that its knowledge will not benefit you in any way, I have no choice but to reveal to you a little of the matter and to give you a few hints and suggestions, since your insistence exceeds all measure.

I want you to know that the abundance of my wealth and the power of my opulence were so great that wise accountants tried in vain to comprehend it. Some time ago I accumulated a large amount of goods, as is customary among merchants and, anticipating profit and gain, went to Qanudj,[3] accepting all the hardships of travel. I was joined by many distinguished merchants who considered it a great honour to belong to a caravan led by myself. It so happened that when we were about four days' travelling distance from Qanudj, I lost contact with the caravan and its cargo of goods and found myself in a wilderness devoid of any human beings. The desert spread out before my eyes was so terrible that I almost lost the courage to continue living. Hurry as I might, first in one direction and then another, wandering aimlessly about from dawn to dusk, I was still unable to escape from that terrible place. Horrifying sounds assailed my ears all the time, making my blood curdle, and again and again strange figures appeared before my eyes, causing me to tremble with fear like the needles on a pine tree. After sunset, when darkness began to spread across the earth, the steppe was turned into a heaving sea before the eyes of my imagination, threatening to devour the heavenly constellations. The branches of the desert shrubs bent low, whipped by a terrible storm, and the vehemence of the gusts set the sand in motion, making it look like Pharaoh's serpents conjured up by his magicians and appearing as if they were about to devour the whole world. Driven by the force of necessity, I placed my heart into the hand of destruction, put the chain of destiny around my neck and lay down under a shrub, expecting death. In my fear and horror it seemed as if my limbs were torn from my body and my bones and sinews were falling apart.

Suddenly the wind carried the sound of distant footsteps to my ears and as I looked around I saw a human being far away, approaching hurriedly. In this deathly wilderness the presence of another human being seemed impossible to me and I thought it must be a Div wanting to kill me or a Ghul bent on taking my life. I quickly crawled into a hole in the ground and hid behind a thorny shrub like a bird about to be killed by a king's falcon in rapid pursuit. I prayed to God for protection. Without any enquiry or question, the man came straight at me and began shouting in a terrible voice: "Who are you and what are you doing in this terrible desert all alone? Are you a Div or a Ghul who lures human beings into his net and takes them into this lonely wilderness to torture them to death?"

I was so horror-stricken that I was unable to utter a word. My teeth began to chatter and I was unable to feel anything or to move, like a body without soul. My silence seemed to fan the flames of his fierce anger, his brow was furrowed with raging fury and he screamed at me: "Speak at once and tell me who you are or my bloodthirsty sword will sever your head from your body!" I tried to reply in my terrible fright and said: "Young man, abandon your wrath! I am a human being; providence has separated me from my camp and I have lost my way in this deathly desert. I am helpless and unable to find my way back to the path of hope. For God's sake, have mercy on me in my desperate plight and extend your helping hand as is customary among generous men. Be like Khizr[5] and guide me so that I may find the way back to my companions and return to my people and my tents."

When the young man learnt the truth about my desperate situation, the clouds of his anger dispersed and goodwill returned to his veins as he said: "Your mind has been racked by fear, but compose yourself because now you have been released from the place of danger. You have raised yourself from the whirlpool of destruction on to the shore of freedom. There is an exceedingly beautiful city not far from here. Its surroundings are so wonderful that, like the Garden of Eden, they will banish all worries from your heart and its inhabitants are like those of paradise. That city is fascinating beyond belief. In its streets a thousand delights are displayed before the stranger's eyes and its houses are of perfect purity like the depth of the mirror. Manes'[6] dwelling is but one of the beautiful places and Farvardin's[7] workshop is only one example of its fresh spring-like nature.

A Garden of Eden surrounds the lush and beautiful
 land
Which extends around Kavzar's banks,[8]
The earth offers nothing but peace
And the glorious place is all purity.
Where the scent of green plants is carried on the
 wind
And joy and well-being exist forever,
A river of gold irrigates its fields,
The earth overflows with saffron.

Since time immemorial the city bore the name of Lubatbaz.[9] I was given the honour of being appointed gatekeeper in that city which makes Iram[10] suspicious and makes paradise envious with its beautiful castles and enchanting houses, with its inhabitants who are like the houris of paradise, and with its delectable gardens. I am called the Rizvan of Lubatbaz.[11] Come, let us hurry and escape from this dangerous desolation as fast as we can and make our way to that city shining in heavenly glory, where you can rest on the cushions of pleasure."

When I saw that he was a man of exceptionally charming manner and delightful courtesy, I blessed him and addressed thanks to God. Then I followed him like his shadow until we reached the gates of the city. The sight of the city's surroundings filled me with wonder and I was certain the very heavens were revealing themselves to me....'

The young stranger had just reached the point of his story when suddenly two cats, which had been fighting and biting each other viciously, dropped from the flat roof above into the midst of the assembled company. Without giving any thought to the mischievous tricks played by fate, the guests had sat and listened intently to the stranger's story. They now jumped up and ran away like frightened chickens when the cats mewed and spat, and in the general confusion the stranger took this opportunity to depart.

When Aziz had recovered from his fright, he was so depressed by the escape of the young man—which had deprived him of the end of the story—that his health began to deteriorate. He sent forth his servants in all directions to search for the man who had disappeared, but they were unable to find any trace of him. He had vanished like the phoenix. Aziz's desire to hear the remainder of the story, and to learn the outcome of the whole affair, soon began to exceed all bounds and his heart was gripped by such powerful longings that he preferred to shake off the peaceful bonds of his life and to commit himself instead to the shackles of restlessness. He therefore decided to prepare for the journey to Qanudj. Although relatives and friends tried to dissuade him, they did not succeed. Aziz took leave of his friends and went forth into the open country, taking with him only a few faithful servants, some reliable slaves and a few bales of merchandise.

In his restless impatience he passed one resting-place after another and soon reached Qanudj without having once broken his journey. From Qanudj he immediately started to search for the city of Lubatbaz, but was unable to find any trace of it. The flame of his longing started burning in his heart more fiercely from day to day and the fire of madness consumed him so utterly that soon he could be likened only to glowing ashes. At last, everything he had brought with him was consumed as a result of his incessant search, and his servants had turned away from him. They parted company and each of them went his own way, as Aziz had lost all power over them. Wrapped in a beggar's cloak, he found himself transplanted from the fertile furrow of companionship into the desolation of loneliness.

He did not know which way to turn and refused even to consider returning home. Whether he liked it or not, he had to endure his poverty and thus he dragged himself, lonely and deserted, searching along the roads and wandering about aimlessly like one possessed, sometimes through towns, at other times across the country, and he crossed mountains and deserts in his mad quest. He squandered the capital of his life on the vain hope of gain—and in so doing gained nothing. On occasions, when he thought of his family, the spark of despair threatened to burn the harvest of his hope and at other times, when he was unable to reach his cherished destination, in his misery he allowed his heart to drain, drop by drop, from the sky of his eyes to the market place of his cheeks.

One day, as he was again wandering about in the desert, uttering a thousand distressed sighs and heart-rending cries, he suddenly met a man of noble appearance whose forehead reflected kindness and from whose face shone the light of mercy. The stranger asked him the reason for his sorrow and confused state and Aziz told him in beautiful and well-chosen words what had happened to him and begged the stranger, who appeared to him like a Khizr, for help and support. The young man replied: 'You, whose reason had been struck by misfortune and whose judgment has been impaired, into what misery have you plunged yourself? It is madness to destroy oneself by roaming the desert and trying to catch the wind in one's hands only on the strength of a stranger's story, without examining the truth of his words. The task you have undertaken cannot be solved. Therefore, choose a road as soon as possible that will bring you greater benefit.'—'Young man,' said Aziz, 'since I am separated from my family and have chosen this path which leads nowhere, how could my soul counsel me to turn back half-way without having found the object of my search? For God's sake do try and give me a helping hand to the best of your ability.'—'Oh, stubborn and unreasonable Aziz,' replied the stranger, 'even if one were to search a whole lifetime one would not be able to retrieve the pearls of existence from the abyss of nothingness. There is no such city as Lubatbaz anywhere on the face of the earth. How, therefore, could you possibly find your way there, even with my help? If you have injured your foot by striking it with a pickaxe, you must at least make sure that the wound does not turn gangrenous. Therefore, while you are still able to do so, decide quickly to catch up with the caravan of life and make sure that you will find shelter in the hostelry of salvation.'

'Young man, you who are able to give such good advice,' said Aziz, 'do you not know that the precious jewel of good advice is worthless to a poor wanderer treading the path of search? For God's sake, show me a little more kindness and do not let me, unfortunate wretch, suffer disappointment as long as the sunlight of goodness shines from your face, and do not let me despair in the dark dust of hopelessness.' To this the stranger replied: 'Oh, you foolish man, follow me quickly so that I may guide you towards the path which may take you to your destination.' Aziz followed his lead and went with him. After walking for some time, they reached a tree; there they stopped and the stranger, pointing in the direction to be followed, said: 'Hurry along this path I have shown you and if you continue in this direction you will not miss your destination. Then you will find your fortune.' Handing Aziz an ivory sword in a scabbard of silk, the stranger said to him: 'If your limbs grow tired from the long journey and you are unable to walk any farther and long for a rest, you must draw this sword and hold it out in front of you; however, as soon as you are ready to continue your journey, you must replace it in the scabbard.' With these words he disappeared from sight.

Aziz did as the young man had advised him and walked on confidently, endeavouring all the time to make good progress. He no longer cared whether his path led uphill or downhill, through thorny shrubs or across stony fields—he gladly and cheerfully accepted the hardships of the journey until the sun, the world-wide messenger, interrupted his journey through the universe and settled down for the night in the west. Then Aziz stopped, withdrew the ivory sword from the scabbard as he had been told and held it in front of him, and at once he saw before him in the lonely desert a large city, which was so beautiful that words cannot describe it. There Aziz took up lodgings in a hostelry, chose a sleeping chamber where he lay down to rest, ate and drank to his heart's content and placed his head upon the pillow of slumber. When the cock crowed in the morning, he put his sword back into the scabbard, the city disappeared and Aziz continued his journey through the desert as on the previous day.

In brief, he continued his journey in this manner, and after travelling for a long time he reached the shores of a lake. He wanted to quench his burning thirst in the waters of the lake but while he was drinking, the belt holding the ivory sword snapped, the sword fell into the water and sank into the depths. Aziz was unable to retrieve it. He was overcome by grief and, deeply depressed and confused, he sat down by the lake and the fortress of his brain was shaken to its very foundations. A short while later, however, he pulled himself together and continued along the path the young man had shown him and thus once again became a wanderer in the desert of grief. After many days he reached a corn field. A farmer was sitting at the edge of the field, enjoying a goblet of wine while his wife was standing nearby sowing seed grain over the field. Aziz wanted to engage the farmer in conversation. He approached courteously, hoping that the farmer would respond in accordance with good manners, and addressed him. The farmer did indeed regard Aziz in a friendly manner and enquired after his well-being. Aziz told him what had happened and revealed to him his innermost wish.

'Handsome young man,' said the farmer, 'what a disastrous idea and what a senseless thought! Do not court disaster in such a stupid manner. Give up your nonsensical plan because it is beyond all the bounds of possibility for a man like you to complete successfully such an undertaking. If you were born under a lucky star, settle down with us and share our company for a while so that you may be safe from the tortures of fate.'

Aziz accepted the offer and rested, in the shade of rural hospitality, from the troubles of his unsuccessful search. At that time strange events began to take place in the farmer's field: every morning, as soon as the dawn breeze started blowing and the first sunrays broke through, a mist would descend, gradually settling like a blanket over a certain tree at the edge of the field. The mist enveloped its leaves and branches while at the same time a light shone through the mist like the burning thorn-bush which Moses saw. Then a hand emerged from the fog, its beauty comparable to that of the white hand of Jesus, and shining with such brightness that the world-illuminating sun could have borrowed some of its glare. The farmer then went up to the tree and, like a trained cup-bearer, gave the hand a beaker of pure wine. The hand then disappeared, only to reappear a short while later to return the empty beaker. This ceremony was repeated daily until the farmer had given out forty beakers of wine. The hand then disappeared for good, the mist started to rise and merged with the clouds. After barely an hour had passed, the fog had dispersed completely.

As chance would have it, the farmer had to go away for some reason or other. He therefore entrusted Aziz with the care of his house and estate and went forth. Upon leaving, he asked Aziz to be quite sure to pass a beaker of rose-coloured wine to the hand from the world beyond, in the prescribed manner. Aziz, who had thereby taken it upon himself to discharge all domestic tasks during the host's absence, fulfilled his duties faithfully and, following the farmer's instructions, served the wine to the hand which appeared from the mist-covered tree and did his best to follow the instructions most carefully. A few days later, however, he felt an irresistible urge to uncover this irksome mystery and to explore the nature of the matter by means of a closer investigation. Finally, he was completely overcome by this absurd desire and one day, while passing the beaker, he suddenly thrust aside all caution and quickly gripped the hand just as it appeared out of the mist, ready to take the beaker of wine. At that moment a cry was heard, so terrible that it would have curdled the blood of a lion, and a mighty bird with powerful claws extended its beak from the blanket of mist, took hold of Aziz as if he were a miserable sparrow and flew high up into the sky with him. Then the bird descended again and settled on the top of a dome. There he released Aziz who rolled down like a ball, landing in a pit so dark that the blackest night could have borrowed some of its gloom. Try as he might to climb up again, he was unable to find the road of hope and he lay there helplessly, waiting at death's door and ready to start his journey into the land of eternity.

Suddenly he noticed a light. A ray of sunlight fell through a hole no larger than a coin. Aziz scratched with his fingernails until he had widened the hole sufficiently for him to look through with one eye. Despair gave him such strength that he succeeded with the greatest of efforts to increase the size of the hole to the point where a man could squeeze through, though with difficulty. After a thousand troubles he finally succeeded in escaping from this terrible confinement.

As it happened, a very sturdy net had been spread at that very point. Aziz immediately fell into the net, which closed round his neck. The more he thrashed about hoping to free himself, and tugged at the net, the more tightly its strands enmeshed his limbs. At that moment a huntsman, who had seen what had happened, came running along in a great hurry. He pulled Aziz out of the net, tied one rope round his neck and another round his leg, and walked with him for a distance of about two miles until they reached a palace of breathtaking beauty, looking like a heavenly fortress. A young woman, beautiful beyond description, put her head out of one of the palace windows, looked at Aziz and said: 'Today the catch is poor. Let him lie until he is in a fit state to be received.' The huntsman released Aziz at once. Aziz, who was downcast by sorrow, felt so miserable and depressed that he did not have the strength to move. Instead, he lay down at once in the shade of the palace, closed his eyes and surrendered to sleep.

When he raised his head from the cushion of slumber, he found himself lying in a desert which extended in all directions as far as the eye could see. Gripped by terror, he began trembling like an aspen leaf and started running about aimlessly in this terrible desert. He was consumed by thirst and all the time he saw before him the spring of life in the form of a mirage and rushed in this or that direction trying to reach it until at long last he stopped near a hill and lay down to rest, exhausted by his strenuous search. As the saying goes:

> The place where the tired man finds his rest, is his fatherland.

Remaining at this hope-destroying place, he expected

the loving comfort of death, since he believed that he had no other way of escape from the dire straits of suffering. At that very moment an old man on horseback came riding from behind the hill. He rode up to Aziz and asked him why he was lying there in this helpless state and why he had given up all hope of survival. After receiving the required information, he presented Aziz, who was nearly dying of thirst, with life-giving water like a Khizr or Messiah and guided him from the desert of despair to the spring of hope. He showed him the way to freedom and directed his steps from the crossroads of confusion to the broad highway of wish fulfilment.

Aziz thanked the venerable old man and followed in the direction he was shown. Despite his weakness he hurried forth with the speed of the east wind. Travelling at the speed of a gentle breeze he walked the whole night to reach the haven of safety. Just as the rose of the morning began to smile through the dawn breeze, he reached a town so magnificent that the beholder stood wide-eyed with amazement at the beauty of its houses. The surroundings resembled the Garden of Eden with its wealth of pleasure and joy. Its air, like the air of heaven, was a delight for the heavenly gatekeeper and the houris. Wonderful rivers flowed everywhere, like the springs of eternal paradise, between deliciously smelling deep-blue flowers. In the branches of the trees sat birds which sang and trilled the tunes of Barbad.[12] Along the banks of the rivers cypresses and plane trees grew side by side with apple and pomegranate trees bent low under the heavy burden of fruit, and emerald-winged parrots sank their beaks into the sweet fruits of the mango trees, sucking like infants at their mothers' breasts. In the scented air the grapes were heavy with the refreshing juices of life, like the wine fermenting in the cask, and the intoxicated trees embraced each other with their branches like flowers.

From the bowels of the earth there rises the perfume
of amber,
Heavenly air surrounds ripe fruit.
The fruit-laden branches bend towards the ground,
They lie humbly in devout prayer.
And the grape swells up boldly like a boaster,
No nation on earth denies my rule.

Feasting his eyes on all these wonders, Aziz lost consciousness for a moment and stood there, speechless and motionless like a statue. When he came to, he started walking towards the city. Soon he reached the gate and saw that both its panels were studded with sparkling jewels. The earth was scented like musk and the streets were paved with agate from the Yemen, and it looked as if the heavens had strewn their seven stars and the meadows their wild roses over them. Aziz entered the gate and found himself in the bazaar, where the tall arches curved towards both sides like the eyebrows of a beautiful woman. They were adorned with a thousand charming pictures and fascinating paintings which filled the beholder with intoxicated admiration. The earth in the city was clear of all shrubs and weeds just as the hearts of the devout are cleansed of all falsehood and dirt. The grieving heart was delighted by the air like the harmonies of song. The city streets made the mind joyful like wine and the inhabitants were gay and happy like the dwellers in paradise.

Aziz stood there, numbed, as if drowning in the sea of amazement, by the sight of this wonderful place, and he thought: 'So much beauty can surely be found only in the Garden of Eden or in the wonderful land of Iram.'—Meanwhile two sprightly young men, blessed with great visible and hidden beauty, came along—their figures like cypresses, their cheeks like roses and with faces whose radiance rivalled the gold of the sun and the silver of the moon. They approached at such speed that the suddenness of their movements, together with the heat of the sun, caused beads of perspiration to form on their glowing faces, like dew-drops on the leaves of jasmin. Each of them took Aziz by one sleeve and they walked away with him swiftly as the wind. Aziz was frightened by the demeanour of the young men and begged them to release him, but the two hurrying guides paid no attention and took him to a castle so beautiful that one corner of its arch alone shone more brightly than all the nine heavens together. The realm's dignitaries and the highest office-bearers of the state were all gathered together in this heavenly palace. A vizier who resembled Asaf,[13] and who sat at the foot of the Solomonic throne, ordered the servant to take Aziz, who was trembling at the sight of such majestic splendour, to the baths. There he was bathed, his body was cleansed of the grime of travel, he was dressed in regal gowns and anointed with sweet-smelling oils, following which a king's crown was placed upon his head and he was lifted on to the jewel-studded throne like a mighty ruler. The nobles of the kingdom and the dignitaries of the realm assembled as his servants around the throne and threw themselves down on the ground as was the court custom, kissed the ground and their cries of 'Long live the king!' rose high up into the clouds.

When Aziz saw all this, he remained seated, speechless like a painting, and for some time he dived into the sea of contemplation and the depths of thought, asking himself: 'Who am I and in what kind of puzzling company do I find myself? If all this splendour is revealed to me only in the land of dreams, why should my eyes once again behold the rose-bed of wakefulness?' The wise minister, guided by the shining light of his reason and under the expert direction of his understanding, found the way into Aziz's state of mind and read the writing of surprise on his forehead. This wise man kissed the foot of the throne with humble lips, saying: 'This city, which is a world full of beauty, whose paths are adorned with a thousand paradise rivers and heavenly springs, and whose inhabitants are tall and beautiful as cypresses and pine trees, is called Lubatbaz. The ruler of this place of Elysian joys was compelled by the eternal law of this world which governs birth and death, to move on into the world of eternity and as he left neither children nor other heirs, he decided at his hour of departure from the gay dwelling places of this world that he who would be the first to arrive the following morning when the sun appeared above the horizon, even if he were the poorest beggar, should be given the king's power and should be placed on the high throne, and the reins of government were to be placed into his strong hands. At the same time there is allotted to him in the sky of his kingdom a veiled moon, a lone pearl in the jewel box of princely glory, a girl so beautiful that the great sun is unable to look into her radiant face except through a veil curtain, the proud cypress is unable to escape from her fascination when she stands facing it in her bewitching slenderness, and the full moon wanes and turns into a moon sail with the desire to kiss her feet. Chastity never leaves her heart, just as a reflection in the mirror never leaves its frame. The order is therefore as follows: if a man has taken his place on the throne of world rule by the grace of fate and with the help of his lucky stars, the most secret chamber of his life shall glow in the candlelight of the cheeks of this heavenly moon; but he must never harbour in his heart the faintest desire for the unattainable princely bride. His hand of desire must stay away from the harvest in the harem of the world's ruler. And now, as your lucky star has reached its zenith and after having guided you from the darkness of destruction to the brightness of a king's dignity, what reason can there be for you to tremble like a quivering arrow and to fall silent and still like a statue? Raise your head from your chest of sorrow, open the eye of hope to the sight of your fortune and enjoy to the full the pleasures of this world.'

On hearing these words, Aziz was filled with joy and delight that defy all description. After enduring so many hardships and having completed so many dangerous journeys, he now sat here in the city of Lubatbaz on the ruler's throne and raised the banner of fortune in the kingdom's camp. The nightingale's song of congratulation was heard from young and old, it even reached the angels of heaven, and the cries of devotion from the tongues of the rich and the poor echoed from the turquoise dome of the sky.

After the public audience, the wise vizier conducted Aziz to the inner chambers and here, where all unrest and disturbance were eliminated, he spread out before Aziz the customs of the ruler's power and the laws of government, explained to him the formulae of exercising his power, the methods of statecraft, the means of compulsion and expression of will and the ways of administering justice.

The following day, after the king of the heavenly bodies

had assumed his seat in the green dome of the sky and poured his light over the audience-chamber of the world, Aziz also mounted the throne of his realm and with the minister's consent he gave orders to prepare for a wedding. Those who prepared the pleasures and spread joy arranged everything necessary for a gay and festive banquet. The breeze of improvised song in the rose-garden of beautiful anticipation freshened, and the wind of cheerfulness carried to the nose of desire the pleasant aroma of fulfilment. The golden wine sparkling in silver crystal cups invited the companions of fortune to partake of the feast of the carefree. The dust of sorrow was flushed away from human hearts by the pure juice of the grape and the singers swept the weeds of sadness away from people's minds with their tunes. The joyous cries of intoxicated men caused Venus to dance on the meadow of the sky.

After the sun had set in the west and the bright moon had climbed up to the throne of the sky, the jewel-studded throne was carried under favourable omens to the secret chambers of happiness and here the beautiful daughter of the fairies was adorned to shine like the sun on the throne of the universe. An abundance of roses covered her head and bosom and an excess of rubies and pearls was sprinkled over her head and feet. The flowers at this feast were so beautiful that they made the spring jealous and the amount of pearls and jewels aroused envy even in the depths of the sea and in the gem-bearing mines.

When the king was due to enter the bridal chamber, rosy-cheeked girls dressed in fine gowns lined up quickly, forming a line from the door of the private chambers to the public audience hall. They captured the heart with their umbra-scented curls and they unfolded their beauty like proud peacocks with a thousand coquettish games, like the flowers of the field and the candles in a festive gathering.

> Thus they played gaily all the evening
> At times bewitching, at times singing magic songs.
> A garland of wavy curls adorned their brows,
> They clapped their hands, dancing gracefully on
> tiptoe.

The king entered, filled with pride and power like the moon in the assembly of stars or the spring on the open fields. Upon beholding the beautiful girls, his face opened like a rose and he hurried towards the most beautiful of them all in her bridal chamber. He placed the whole world as a bridal gift at the feet of the radiant daughter of the sun and when he saw the rose-gardens of her beauty, he was filled with joy. After these two noble persons had sat down on the high seat of friendship, united on one throne, they looked like two cypresses rising from the same lawn or sun and moon fusing their light into a single heavenly sign. The throne glowed in thousandfold splendour like the fiery heavens themselves, while the girls closed the circle around the throne like stars. Joy flowed from the corridors of the palace like water from a spring, and gaiety fell from the pillars of the palace like rain from the clouds.

At the mere sight of this enchantress, radiant in heathen beauty, Aziz completely lost his heart and faith. He sat in her chamber, he placed her round his neck like a garland of flowers and he hid in her embrace like in a cloak. At times he would kiss her moon face and at other times her cheeks that put the sun to shame, sometimes he would drink the wine of life from the cup of her sweet ruby lips, then he would hold her in an embrace as tight as a bound bouquet of jasmin until the breeze of desire began to pulse through his veins and sparks arose from the forge of his heart, and he was overcome by the desire to pluck the rose of his will from the bush of hope.

The beautiful woman was afraid that he might break the hidden bud and thought of ways and means of preventing the nightingale's sharp beak from tearing to pieces the tender jasmin leaf. The king was unable to control his passion and he tried to achieve his aim with the help of the cup. He took from the cup-bearer's hand a goblet full of wine, intending to make the beautiful woman more willing and to lure the phoenix into his trap. The fairy, who had grown up in a climate of wine and song, allowed herself to be lured by the delicious drink. Intoxicated with gaiety, she curved her body like the slender cypress. Carried away by the festive revelry, she jumped up, the musk-scented chains of her curls coiled like letters over the pages of her moon-bright cheeks; an umbra-scented garland of light surrounded her sun face. Experienced in cunning, she personally filled the gold-inlaid beaker with noble, invigorating wine. The man-felling drink was then mixed with rose water and she handed it to the king as a token of love. The king, robbed of all senses by his ecstasy, took the beaker and drained it to the last drop. With artful gaiety she allowed the sweet wine to cloud his mind and reason to escape from his brain. She ordered the sun-cheeked jokers and the fairy-like maidens to hurry along and enliven the banquet hall with dancing and string music and kindle the lamp of music with the flame of their voices. One of them performed cartwheels around the glowing beauties with such skill that the heavenly wheel stood still with surprise and remained motionless like the pole star. Another rose into the air with astonishing ease and skill where, floating like a fairy, she clapped hands and feet together. Another drove reason out of people's hearts with the fiery rhythm of her clapping hands, while yet another enchanted her listeners by the wonderful modulation and the sweet richness of her songs.

A universe like the bright seat of dreams,
The flashing thoughts of tempting imagination.
Every lip red like a tulip in the garden,
Offering itself freely like spring in Khuzistan.[14]
From zenith to nadir could be heard
The enchanting sound of girls' clear-voiced song.

The king was so enraptured by the sight of the beautiful young girls that he lost sway over his will; finally he was completely overcome by the effects of the wine and placed his head upon the cushion of sleep, leaving the flower-bud of his wishes standing untouched in the field of hope.

When the bride of the morning had risen from the bed of night and the blue sky had drunk its morning wine from the beaker of sun, Aziz, whose lucky star was darkened, was awakened by the morning breeze and torn from his carefree slumber. He looked around in all directions and no longer found the shining sun, nor a trace of the gay feast of the night before. As in the past, he found himself lying in the terrible desert, threatened by the perils of loneliness and enmeshed in the net of poverty. Thinking of his beloved and the happiness that had been given to him, and of the beautiful evening feast, he covered his head with ashes, as is customary among those stricken by ill-luck.

Then he involuntarily resumed his wanderings, hoping that the escaped water would once again fill the river-bed of happiness. He had barely walked one mile when, to his surprise, he suddenly saw the walls of his home town Audjin. This sight plunged him into the bottomless depths of astonishment, but sorrow mingled with his surprise and he shed oceans of tears.

As there was nothing else for him to do, he returned to his house, distributed the rest of his belongings among the needy and issued letters of release to his slaves. Then he left his family, wrapped himself in ash-grey garments, placed a fur over his shoulders like a madman[15] and joined the fraternity of the insane by taking up his domicile in the desert which had never been trodden by man's foot; for the rest of his life he drank the poison of suffering from the beaker of love, drove the diamond splinter of misery deep into his heart and tossed on the bed of grief. With a tortured mind and half-blinded by tears, he spent his life in the company of wild animals until his last hour in which, in the bitterness of his death struggle, he paid the last few pennies of his life to Death, the relentless creditor, with the name of his beloved on his lips.

18. THE DOG WITH THE RUBY NECKLACE

KING AZADBAKHT of Constantinople once related the following story: By the grace of God—glory be to him—and with his help, I ascended the throne of kingly power and assumed the high seat of happiness at a very early age, after my father had left this mortal world for the eternal realm; thereafter the kingdom of Rum[1] was like wax under my signet ring.

Shortly after I came to the throne a merchant from Badakhshan[2] arrived in my country, bringing with him innumerable valuable goods and immeasurable quantities of gems and cloth. The rumour of his arrival spread through the land and reached my ears as well. I therefore gave orders for him to be brought before me. I wanted to hear from him about the activities of the kings in other countries and to learn about the way of life and the qualities of mighty sultans and prominent chieftains. The widely-travelled and experienced man arrived and humbly presented me with a small box. When I opened it I found that it contained a ruby of utmost purity, weighing one mithkal.[3] I had never seen anything like it in my father's treasury, nor had I ever heard anyone speak of such a stone. The present pleased me greatly and I regarded it as a good omen. I bestowed great honours upon the man, gave him presents and granted him the right to wear a robe of honour. In addition, I issued him with letters patent exempting him from all taxes and dues within the boundaries of my realm.

He remained at my court for some time. He was a wise man who knew much about the good and bad sides of human nature. He was also very eloquent and knowledgeable about traditions and customs and I benefited from his company as much as I had hoped I would.

To be brief, I valued my ruby so much and regarded it as such an incomparable gem that I had it brought out almost every day when I was holding audience, so that poor and rich could look at it. There I sat, playing with the ruby, and all the people around me had to praise it. One day, ambassadors from many countries had gathered at my court to pay their respects, and I had arranged for a great feast. The Emirs of the realm and the other dignitaries had taken their seats and the servants and my whole retinue from far and near were lined up in rows. I had given orders for a regal banquet to be prepared and for the gates of joy to be opened. As was my habit, I sent for the ruby to have it admired. The ambassador from the Frankish kingdom smiled when he saw my eagerness.

I had a vizier, a very wise man who had held the same office under my father's reign and who now served me with equal skill. The vizier spoke the usual introductory words of praise, and continued: 'With your majesty's permission, I should like to make a few relevant observations.'—'Speak,' I said. The vizier went on: 'It ill becomes one of the mightiest kings ruling over the peoples of the world to brag in this manner about a precious stone, before acquaintances and friends, incomparable though the stone may be. The true value of this gem may perhaps be illustrated by the fact that a merchant in the city of Nishapore in Khorasan has had twelve such rubies, each weighing seven mithkal, set into the collar of a dog.'

His harsh words kindled the flames of my anger. I refused to believe what he said about the merchant in Khorasan, and in my rage I ordered the vizier to be punished by death and his property to be confiscated. At this, the ambassador from the Frankish kingdom rose to plead on the vizier's behalf, and said: 'Mighty king, please tell me, what crime has this old man committed?' —'What crime is uglier than an infamous lie?' I asked. 'Oh king,' he continued, 'how can you be sure that his words are lies?' I replied: 'How can a reasonable person believe that a merchant, who risks his life for profit by crossing deserts and mountains, traversing the Red Sea and Oman, would place twelve rubies, each of them weighing seven mithkal, round the neck of a dog?' The ambassador kissed the ground and spoke again: 'Oh king, may the realm remain in your hand for ever! Fate is capricious and life goes up and down from day to night and the change of times is without end. Any report you receive may be true or false. Both possibilities exist. It may be that the vizier's account is true, improbable as it may sound. And if he should indeed have told a lie, with the best of intentions, please remember that

> The king considers the things reflected in the words of viziers,
> And their advice seals the fate of the world.

The day may come when all noblemen will be forced to mourn the fact that your majesty ordered an old and well-meaning servant to be executed because he said something which had not been proved untrue, forgetting what you owed this man in return for many years of faithful service. Earlier kings had prisons built where they could lock up for a few days anyone who had angered them or aroused their distrust, until their anger had passed or the man's innocence had been proven—so that there was no risk of the king spilling innocent blood.'

In this manner the ambassador tried to calm my anger with words of wisdom and in any other way possible, until he finally persuaded me not to kill the vizier. 'Very well,' I said, 'I will stay his execution for the time being. In response to your plea I will have him imprisoned and grant him one year's grace. If it is proved by then that he has spoken the truth I will spare his life, otherwise I shall know how to deal with him.' The ambassador kissed the ground and was satisfied with what I had said. The vizier was sent to prison.

When news of this reached the vizier's household, they all burst into tears and lamented bitterly. The vizier had a daughter, a clever and intelligent girl of seventeen, who could read and write and was very talented. Her father had set up special quarters for her next to his harem, had given her beautiful girls as companions and servants and had made sure that she had everything necessary for a life of luxury. He also provided her with games to pass the time. The beautiful young girl had spent happy days and nights together with other Emirs' daughters. On this day, too, the most beautiful of all the beautiful girls of her time was surrounded by the pleasures and joys of life, when suddenly her mother burst in, bare-headed and barefoot, with dishevelled hair, and with bitter tears in her bloodshot eyes. She beat her daughter's face with her fists and cried: 'Oh God, would that daughters were never born—and if they were, would that they were not granted a long life. Oh how I wish that I had a son instead of you, even if he were blind! At least I would not have to mourn, because even so he would certainly remove in this hour the stains of suffering from my soul and release the knot tied by the hand of fate.'

The daughter tried to calm her mother with loving

words, and asked: 'What has happened? What is the reason for your despair and this pitiful lament? And what could a blind son do for you that I could not?'

'Dust and ashes upon your head!' replied the mother. 'What greater misfortune could befall us than that your father be thrown into jail by the king? He did this only because your father said that there is a merchant at Nishapore in Khorasan who has placed twelve rubies, each of them weighing seven mithkals, round the neck of his dog. The king regarded this statement as a lie and at once gave orders for your father to be executed. However, after the ambassador from the Frankish kingdom had pleaded on his behalf, the king ordered your father to be sent to prison and gave him one year's grace so that the truth of his words may be proved; otherwise the death penalty will be carried out. If you had been a son you would have travelled to Khorasan without hesitation, to bring that merchant before the king so that your old father may be free again.'

'With all due respect for your words,' said the daughter, 'divine destiny cannot be changed. In the hour of calamity we must exercise patience and submit to God's will so that happy days may return. Your crying and lamenting cannot benefit us in any way; it may well be that our enemies would inform the king of your conduct, in a manner suitable for their plans, so that you would thereby be provoking the king's wrath even further. No, as far as the blows of fate are concerned, there is no other remedy but patience and just as the prophet says: "Patience is the key to joy." As for restoring the liberty of my unhappy old father, we must place our trust in God because we are all His slaves and the children of His slaves and whatever the Lord may command, right is always in His hand.'

The wise girl thus tried to make her mother see reason again with good advice and sincere words of comfort. She herself rolled up the cloth of life's joy and withdrew into the dark corner of oblivion. At night, however, she called her nurse, who was her confidante and helpmeet in important matters and in charge of the entire household, and spoke to her in complete privacy. She addressed her with sweet and tempting words and promised her many things, following which she took her into her confidence and revealed her secret plans: 'In order that I may restore my father's freedom and undo the disgrace that has befallen my mother, I shall, with God's help and assistance, travel to the land of Iran in your company. With the loving aid of the people of Khorasan and important men in Nishapore, I intend to obtain a reliable report on the whole matter and to rescue my father from prison and death.'

The nurse refused for a long time. When she saw, however, that the girl was determined to carry out her plan, she considered the matter. Finally it was decided that the nurse should secretly gather goods suitable for Persia and Khorasan, as well as precious gems and other things, and that they should procure a sufficient number of slaves and companions and prepare everything else that might be required on a journey. After these plans had been put into effect by the successful efforts of the nurse, the girl donned men's clothes and took with her gems and valuable goods in such quantities that it would have taken an ordinary person a whole lifetime to accumulate them. Accompanied by her trusted servants and heavily laden camels, she left the house in the darkness of night at the appointed hour in complete secrecy. On the instructions of the supposed merchant, the caravan moved off on the journey to Persia, richly laden with its bales of goods.

When the girl's mother learned what had happened, she kept her daughter's flight secret for fear of disgrace.

In the meantime, the supposed merchant's son, favoured by good luck, reached the city of Nishapore fit and well after a long journey, and together with his companions took up quarters at the merchants' inn where they rested for a day and a night. The following morning, the disguised young girl went to the baths and scrubbed herself thoroughly clean, then put on men's clothes again and with a face radiant as the sun and a heart full of hope, she went to the bazaar of Nishapore. Whilst walking about gracefully between the stalls of the bazaar, she noticed the shop of a jeweller where all kinds of gems were poured out in an enormous heap, as though they were grain. Inside the shop sat a man of perhaps forty years, with the expression of a dignified father on his face, dressed in a splendid gown and leaning back on his brocade cushions. A large number of slaves and servants with gold-covered hats and jewel-studded belts were lined up in rows and in front of the shop a few noblemen sat on chairs talking to the owner.

The supposed young man was surprised at this and said to himself: 'This must be the merchant my father has spoken of.' And while she prayed to God that he may give her an opportunity to prove the truth of her father's words, she looked around and saw another shop adjoining the first one. There were neither goods nor articles of use to be seen there, but only two steel cages. In each of them sat a man in irons. Their hair and beards reached as far as their belts, and their fingernails were as long as the claws of a wild beast. There they sat, with dust in their hair, devoid of all emotion, their hollow cheeks full of terror, their bodies seemingly consisting only of skin and bones. Never before had anything similar been seen on the face of the earth, nor had the angry heavens heard of anyone suffering as cruelly as these two. The doors of the cages were bolted and two fierce negro slaves kept watch in front of them.

Amazed and immersed in thought, she pronounced these words: 'There is no power and no might but that of God.'[4] And as she looked in the other direction she saw another shop whose floor was covered with a silk carpet; on it stood a jewel-studded chair with a cover and a golden chain. On the cover lay a dog with a necklace richly adorned with jewels, tied to the chair by the golden chain. At the foot of the chair stood a bowl of water, and two Frankish slave boys, beautiful as the moon, stood nearby in attendance; one held a golden fly-swat in his hands and the other wiped the dust from the dog's head with a cloth woven with gold. The supposed merchant's son looked closer and noticed that there were twelve great rubies on the dog's necklace. She thanked God and began to consider how she could best bring the chair in all its glory to Rum as proof, so that her father might be set free.

In the meantime, the people walking about in the bazaar had noticed the figure of the supposed merchant's son, and on beholding the radiant beauty of his rosy cheeks their hearts and souls were set aflame. Everyone who gazed upon the sun-like beauty of this creature born under a lucky star, stopped, confused and speechless, full of longing to gaze on such a face. They were all filled with the sight of the flowerbed of tulip cheeks, so that the number of onlookers blocked the flow of passers-by. When the merchant noticed that the people in the bazaar kept revolving around this one point like a pair of dividers, he sent one of his slaves out to invite the stranger to come nearer. As soon as the merchant beheld the radiant beauty of the supposed merchant's son, the arrow of love and friendship shot from the arch of the stranger's eyebrows and pierced the merchant's heart. She approached to kiss the merchant's hand and he opened his arms, hugging her as a dear friend, gave her a fatherly kiss on the forehead and invited her to sit down by his side. After the customary courtesies had been exchanged, he asked her: 'Young rose, from what garden do you come? And where are you thinking of going?'

'I was born in Constantinople,' she replied, 'my father was a merchant in his youth but now, after having reached the age of seventy and his eyes having become weak, he is obliged to stay within his four walls, unable to undertake any journeys. For that reason he sent me out and as I feared the hardships of a sea voyage, I travelled to Persia. After my arrival in this country I heard many people praise your virtuous life and your noble character and I desired to meet you in person. This is how I came to Khorasan. I would like to give thanks to God for allowing me to kiss your hands after having reached my destination.'

She thus addressed the merchant with charming words and he replied, visibly moved: 'That was most kind of you. You have endured much trouble and now are cordially welcome here. I am overjoyed by your arrival. But tell me, my son, where are your people? Please do me the honour of moving into my humble house. I do not like the idea of you and your servants living in a strangers' inn. I do enjoy, God be praised, a certain reputation here and although I am but a lowly grain of dust, I have as a result of my kind deeds gained a certain degree of protection, so that my relatives and friends are safe from intervention by the king's authorities and from annoyance by the people and attacks by evil men. It would make me very happy indeed if you were to direct your steps to my house.'

At first the young girl in disguise declined, but finally she agreed and ordered her slaves to take their belongings to the merchant's house, with the help of his servants. She herself remained in the bazaar until the evening, immersed in conversation with the merchant, so that they grew to know each other well. When they were about to go to the merchant's house in the evening, she noticed that one of the two young slaves took the dog in his arms, the other carried the dog's chair and so they walked along, followed by the merchant. They entered the merchant's house and settled down in the hall. At the front of the hall on the side opening out towards the lake, the slaves spread out a carpet and placed the dog's chair on it. Then they began to wait upon and look after the dog. The two cages were also brought in and placed on one side of the hall.

The merchant welcomed the young girl to his house and asked her to make herself at home. He ordered wine to be brought, drank some himself and, in accordance with custom, handed the beaker to the supposed merchant's son. They talked together for a while and when they began to feel merry, food was brought in. Following a signal from the merchant, the slaves placed some of the food before the dog, after spreading a golden cloth in front of its chair. The dog jumped down from the chair, ate as much as it liked and drank water from a golden bowl. Then it jumped back on the chair and laid down to rest while the slave-boys dried its paws and nose with a cloth. In the meantime the two negro slaves took the food and the bowl and placed them in front of the cages. After having received the keys from their master, they opened the cages, drove the two prisoners out with whips and forced them to eat the food left by the dog. Then they were once again locked up in their cages and the keys were returned to their master.

Meanwhile, the meal for the merchant and his guest was also made ready. The young girl felt miserable as a result of having witnessed such inhuman treatment. She found it impossible to believe that the merchant was a follower of the true faith and she therefore did not want to share his meal. No matter how much the merchant urged her to take some of the dishes, she refused to touch any food. When he enquired about the reason for her lack of appetite, she replied: 'With the best will in the world I could not bring myself to eat any of your food. What kind of a life do you lead? First of all, as far as the adherents of the true faith are concerned the dog is an unclean animal—except for the infidel Franks, who are even dirtier than dogs, and even they do not worship their dogs to such an extent. And is it not more than enough that you prevent the two creatures of God from serving the Lord day and night, keeping their eyes from the sight of God? And on top of this you lock them up in such an inhuman fashion, forcing them to eat the food left over by the dog. Tell me truthfully, what religion permits such conduct? After all, the life of all men is in God's hand. You do not act as befits a Muslim; you are weak in your faith and you even worship the most wretched of all animals.'

'My son,' replied the merchant, 'your words weigh heavily on my mind. I know very well that all this does not look pleasant but I am unable to alter things, because fate has decreed that I act in this manner. People view my conduct with revulsion and for a long time I was accused of being a dog-worshipper, but I can swear to you by the Almighty God that I wish nothing but damnation upon the heads of all heathens and infidels!' He recited the creed and reassured his guest about his orthodoxy.

She then wanted to question the merchant more closely about this strange state of affairs, but he said: 'Yes, my son, I have been called a dog worshipper, but I have sworn a solemn oath that I will never reveal to anyone the reason for my action. For a long time I had to pay double or even tenfold taxes in this city to avoid being forced to reveal my secret. My son, if I were to tell you my story, it would only bring you sadness and sorrow. So do not ask me about something which you would gain nothing by knowing about.'

The girl listened to his words and since she considered that her true intentions were connected with the state of affairs as they now came to be recognized, she preferred to refrain from probing more deeply into the matter and, reassured, she began to eat.

The girl was both wise and determined, and stayed in the merchant's house for two months; their relationship became like that between father and son. She captivated his heart completely by her noble appearance and exceptional beauty; indeed, she enchanted him to such an extent that if she disappeared from his sight for only a moment, he felt as if darkness had been cast over his life.

One day, however, while they were drinking together, she began to cry bitterly. The merchant begged her to tell him why she was crying. 'My father,' she exclaimed, 'what can I say? If only I had never entered your house! Then I would not have to suffer the pain of separation, nor to taste despair in the bitter sorrow of parting. I shall have to leave you, without knowing whether I shall ever have the good fortune of meeting you again.'

When the unhappy merchant, who loved her so much, heard these words, he also began to weep, and said: 'Forget this unhappy thought! Is not Persia a beautiful country, too? Our climate is just as pleasant as that of Rum. If you have any relatives there I will send my trusted servant, whom you also trust, together with a number of reliable companions to bring your relatives safely to this country. My son, I have suffered great sorrow in my lifetime; my fate has taken me through many countries and cities and now I have grown old. I possess unlimited money and wealth, but I have neither children nor family and it is therefore my greatest desire that you shall be a son to me, and that as long as I live you shall be the light of my eyes. You shall take care of my business and one day, when my last hour has struck, you will take me to my last resting place.'

'My father,' replied the supposed merchant's son, 'how pleased I should be if I did not have to leave you, but does one not offer pleasure to God by wishing to bring joy to one's parents? My parents are old and frail. They have allowed me to travel for only one year and they are longing for my return. I do not want them to accuse me of disobedience. Neither would you think it right for me to invite such an accusation. But if you were to grant me your kind and fatherly permission to go forth and travel to Rum, I swear that I shall obey your commands for the rest of my life.'

After they had discussed the matter at length, the merchant, who felt himself bound to the supposed merchant's son by the ties of love, decided that the only thing for him to do was to go on the journey, too, although he did not know the way.

And so it was decided that the journey should be undertaken and the necessary preparations were made. When the merchants of Khorasan and Irak heard that the dog-worshipping merchant was about to travel to Rum, a large number of them decided to accompany him. The merchant left the city of Nishapore at an auspicious hour, taking with him enormous quantities of treasure and jewels and a vast number of servants. He established his camp with tents and equipment just beyond the city. The other merchants, together with their goods and belongings, joined the caravan, each according to the extent of his wealth. After they had all assembled, the merchant's slaves brought along a hundred mules laden with cloth, one hundred camels laden with jewels and a further hundred camels carrying gold and silver. They were followed by one hundred young men from Kiptchak, brave men with hearts of warriors and armed with swords, and also by a large number of beautiful slaves with golden belts, who rode on horseback. At the head of the caravan rode the beautiful young girl by the side of the merchant, and their friends formed a circle round her; she was so beautiful that her head shone with the beauty of Venus and her appearance radiated light like the seven stars. On the back of a high-humped young camel was mounted a sedan chair, and there the dog sat under a sunshade. The cages holding the two wretched prisoners had also been loaded on to a camel. And so the caravan started its journey.

When they had reached the last stopping place before Constantinople, the supposed merchant's son asked for permission to ride ahead into the city to arrange quarters for the merchant and his friends. The merchant agreed reluctantly and only on condition that the young girl would not stay away for more than one night. She then rode into the city unaccompanied, reached the house of her parents at night and hurried into the harem. The vizier's servants were speechless at the impertinence of this strange man, but she went straight to her mother, who at first heaped reproach upon her head but then asked what had happened to her on her travels.

'Dear mother,' replied the daughter, 'as God is my witness, what I have done deserves nothing but praise. I have acted purely with the aim of releasing my father from jail and now, God be praised, I have reached the goal of my hopes by the mercy of heaven and thanks to your prayers. The evening of sorrow has now been followed by the morning of joy. I have brought with me both the merchant and the dog with the jewel-studded necklace and all I ask now is your permission to settle this matter tomorrow and to bring about my father's release from prison and death.'

The mother was beside herself with joy at seeing her daughter again and hearing her news. She flung herself on the ground with the most fervent prayers; then she hugged her daughter and blessed her and gave her the permission she had asked for. The following morning the girl went out to meet the merchant. He, urged on by the fever of longing, had started at about the same time, for

It is hard to behold the empty bed of the beloved.

They met about a mile outside the city and there they selected a pleasant, cool site to pitch their tents and rested until the appointed hour of their entry into the city.

One of my chief huntsmen returning from the hunt happened to pass that very place in the late afternoon. The merchant and the supposed merchant's son, together with the other members of the caravan, had just risen from their siesta and were sitting outside the tents on the bank of the gently flowing river, engrossed in conversation. The huntsman wondered who the strangers might be. 'The king has not ordered any of his Emirs to go out as his courier,' he thought, 'and no foreign ambassador has recently been reported.' He therefore told his servant to go along and make enquiries. When the servant approached the caravan, the merchant called him to his tent and asked him about his master's state of affairs. As soon as he had learned the rank of the master of the hunt, he sent a messenger to him with the following invitation: 'If you are willing to share the company of humble people, please show us strangers the kindness of allowing your light to shine on our camp.'

The huntsman, curious to find out who these strangers might be, accepted at once. After exchanging courtesies, the huntsman sat down on a chair and looked at all the animals, servants, masters and the whole display of wealth and the sun-like radiance of the supposed merchant's son. When he noticed the dog sitting on its chair and the two cages, he stood there speechless with surprise. The merchant entertained his guest with great charm, and then ordered a few gowns and valuables to be handed to him as a present. After the huntsman had enquired about the merchant's state of affairs and had learned his name and homeland, he returned to the city.

The following day the huntsman came to my palace and told a few of my Emirs what he had seen. They were greatly surprised about what they had learned. On entering the audience chamber, they told me what they had heard and described the loathsome conduct of the merchant so vividly that the flames of anger were kindled in my breast. I considered that the man was a heathen. For the sake of preserving the purity of the faith it would be necessary to punish him and to issue a stern warning to the other barbarians in this caravan. I therefore ordered a few soldiers to bring me his head and to confiscate his entire property. It so happened that the same Frankish ambassador was present that day who had earlier pleaded on behalf of the vizier, and on hearing my orders he smiled involuntarily. This really inflamed me, because

> If a smile cannot offer me consolation
> I'd rather see tears than smiles.

'You fool,' I said to him, 'what are you laughing about?' —'Oh king,' he replied, 'I am laughing for several reasons. The first is that it is now evident that your vizier, the good counsellor of a great ruler, has spoken the truth and that the unhappy, innocent man must now be released from prison. Praise be to God that my humble plea did prevent your Majesty from spilling innocent blood that day! The second reason is that the most illustrious monarch has given orders for the merchant to be executed without hearing him first and without examining the whole case, simply and purely on the testimony of only one person.

> If you are willing to base your judgment on gossip
> Faith and your realm will soon be lost.
> He who listens to envious speech alone,
> Will never see the heavenly gardens.'

When this honest and well-meaning man had thus given me food for thought and had drawn my attention to the case of the vizier, I gave orders for the merchant, and the one thought to be his son, to be taken to the palace together with the two imprisoned men and the dog. And so, to keep the story short, the soldiers brought them along and after they had been given leave to appear before me, the merchant and his son were presented. Both had donned magnificent gowns and the radiant beauty of the merchant's son shone over my court and dazzled the onlookers.

This exceedingly beautiful creature held in her hands a golden vessel filled with gems of the most exquisite colours. After she had placed the gift at the foot of my throne and had respectfully kissed the ground, she stood aside. The merchant, too, kissed the ground and after pronouncing a blessing for me with an eloquent tongue and well-chosen words, he also stood aside.

I then said to him: 'You Satan in human disguise, you are God's enemy! What intrigues have you hatched out and what snares have you set up? To what nation do you belong and what is your faith?'

'Oh king,' he replied, 'long may your life and your power last! I believe in God and the Prophet Muhammad Mustapha, may God be merciful to him and his family and his companions! I believe in the twelve Imams[5]—peace be with them—and I observe the rules of praying and fasting. If I have come to appear in a suspicious light in the eyes of the people, this is due to causes which I cannot reveal. Oh king! To hide the sufferings of my heart and in order not to expose the sad circumstances, I have accepted the degradation of becoming known as a dog-worshipper and for a long time I had to pay a special tax in Iraq and Khorasan, and now after having placed my head at your majesty's feet I submit to whatever fate may be in store for me.'

My anger rose and I said to him: 'You werewolf of the desert! I am not so stupid as to be fooled by your excuses and evasions. You must either explain to me the cause of your conduct, giving sound reasons that can be accepted by intelligent people, or else you will be condemned to death so that your fate may serve as an example to the others.'

'Your majesty,' he resumed, 'I beg you to spare my life, burdened as it is with suffering. Confiscate all my fortune, my wealth is so great that all the world's accountants together are unable to measure it, but grant me and this young man liberty.'

On hearing these words my temper rose again. 'Banish such idle thoughts from your head,' I said angrily. 'I will not grant you liberty under any conditions except the ones I mentioned, failing which I will make sure that you are put to death.'

He sighed deeply and a flood of tears burst from his eyes. With laments and cries he looked at the rosy-cheeked girl and said: 'My child, if I have to die now, whom shall I entrust with your care?'—'Fool,' I shouted, 'make your choice quickly and do not attempt to mislead me with idle words and empty phrases!'

When the man saw that he had no choice, he stood up before me and said: 'Your Majesty, were my life not threatened and were I not liable to be parted by death from a human being I love beyond all measure, I would never have told my story to anyone. But since I now find myself in this predicament, I beg you to give orders for the two men in their cages, who may seem to be the victims of my cruelty, to be brought here. They, too, should hear my story and bear witness to my truthfulness.'

I consented and ordered the two prisoners to be released

from their cages and to be made to stand on the left and right of the merchant. The merchant, having made his decision, started speaking:

The Story of the Merchant and His Two Brothers

'Your majesty, this man on my right is my eldest brother, the one on my left is the second, and I am the youngest. We come from Persia where our father was a merchant who had invested a capital of eight thousand tomans in trade. My father died when I was fourteen years old. The funeral ceremonies were completed and ten days later my brothers came to me one evening and said: "Choose someone from our family as your confidante so that we may divide our father's money. Each of us can then use his share as he thinks best." I was not prepared to agree to this and said: "Dear brothers, what are you saying? Let me be only one of your faithful servants. Our father has entered in God's peace but you are alive and should therefore look after me in father's place. After all, I am still a child and in need of your care. Thank God, I shall not want for food and clothing."—"This is a clever scheme," they scoffed, "with this trick you could soon make all of us into beggars." I did not reply to their words but threw myself on to my bed and cried. Finally I tried to console myself with the thought that my brothers merely wanted to test me.

Next morning my brothers went out early and at breakfast time the judge's guards came to fetch me. When I was brought before the judge I found my brothers there who repeated their demands of the previous evening. The judge turned to me and asked why I resisted the rule of law. I repeated what I had said the night before. My brothers replied: "If your words are true and your heart and your tongue speak the same language, then you must sign a declaration to this effect to which the seal of law can be affixed. Should you, at a later date, present us with a demand for your inheritance, it shall be devoid of any legal basis."

I believed that my brothers wanted such a written declaration to make sure that in my inexperience I would not squander my inheritance. I therefore signed the document in accordance with their wishes, and the seal of law was affixed to it, whereupon I handed it over to them and went home without the slightest suspicion of treachery in my heart. A few days later, however, my brothers sent a messenger to me with this information: "You must look for another dwelling place. We do not want you to stay in our house any longer." Then I realized that they were out to cheat me. However, I trusted in God and wished them all the best, asking them to give me two days' grace just to put my affairs in order.

During my father's lifetime he used to bring me some kind of present each time he came home from one of his journeys. One of those presents was a slave girl. I sold all my belongings for a total of one thousand toman. With this money I bought everything needed in a household and then, together with my domestic companions, I moved to a new house. Among the things my brothers allowed me to take with me was a dog, whose story was as follows: One day my father brought this dog home from one of his journeys. It had befriended my father's horses and accompanied them everywhere. After some time the dog had puppies and one of them appeared so sweet to me in its clumsy helplessness that I grew very fond of it. I played with it and fed it. When I left my father's house, I wanted this animal to share everything with me. Whereas my brothers had proved ungrateful and cruel to me, the dog became my faithful companion.

After I had set up house, I bought two slaves to serve me. The remainder of the money was intended to be my investment capital. I rented a shop at Kaisariya[6] and, placing my trust in God, I engaged in trade. While my brothers had treated me cruelly and had thrown me out, God took me into his care and bestowed such favours upon me that my capital increased to four thousand toman in the course of three years. I soon became a well respected man among the merchants and I was able to count great and noble people among my customers.

One Friday, in the fourth year after my arrival in the city, I was sitting in my house. One of my slaves had gone to the bazaar to buy a few household requirements. He came back crying. I asked him the reason for his tears and he replied, accusingly: "What do you care for others? All you think about is enjoying life."—"Are you possessed by an evil spirit?" I exclaimed.—"Do you think it is worse," he replied, "to be possessed by an evil spirit than to sit complacently like yourself amongst all these riches and splendours while your two elder brothers have fallen into the hands of a Jew? They owe him one hundred toman and he is having them flogged in the open market square; to make matters worse, the Jew is laughing at them and saying: 'I know that I will never get my money back and this is why I want you to be beaten up well and truly—and one day I will receive my reward in paradise!' And no one is making the slightest attempt to protect them from the Jew."

When I heard this report I felt as if I were drowning

in a sea of sorrow and, beside myself with impatience, I hurried from the house, ordering my slaves to follow me with the money. On arrival at the market square I saw the two young men in the condition as described to me. At this sight I lost control over myself and, shedding bitter tears, I sent the governor's henchmen[7] away with a handful of gold coins, went up to the Jew and said: 'Why do you ill-treat two of God's servants in this manner on a holy day?" The Jew replied: "If you want to protect them, pay me first what they owe me instead of standing there and talking nonsense; otherwise you can keep your jokes about my ill-treatment to yourself."—"How much are you owed? Bring me the promissory note," I said. "They owe me one hundred toman," he replied, "and the note is in the hands of the court."

I paid the hundred toman and the note was handed over to me. I ordered my slaves to carry the two young men, who were lying there in a most miserable state, naked and crying with feet beaten sore, into my house. There I arranged for their wounds to be treated and after they had recovered, I gave them splendid clothes and sent them to the baths. I showed them hospitality and made them welcome in my house. In order not to shame them, I did not say a word about the money left by our father. In view of the humiliation they had suffered, they on their part remained in my house all the time.

After a short while I began to fear that life with me would become too boring for them. One evening, as we were sitting together talking, I said to them: "Dear brothers, it has occurred to me that you should perhaps undertake a journey because a merchant gains respect and esteem through travelling." They agreed and I made all the necessary preparations, spending one hundred toman on each for buying the equipment needed for their journey. I found them a place in a caravan which was due to depart for Turkistan, and advanced them sufficient money to enable them to pay for the hire and care of their riding and load-bearing animals, as well as for other travelling expenses.

Some time had passed since their departure and I waited day and night to see them return safe and well. A whole year went by before the caravan returned, but without my brothers. When I asked several members of the caravan about my brothers, I received a different answer from each of them, but finally I found an honest man who told me: "One of your brothers gambled away all his possessions in Bokhara and then started working in a gambling place. The other befriended the son of an innkeeper and after he had wasted all his money on his friend, he became a waiter in the tavern. The members of the caravan were ashamed to tell you the truth and this is why each has told you some different, silly story."

These words filled me with such sadness and restlessness that I did not know what do with myself. I was unable to eat or sleep. Without letting any of my neighbours know what I was doing, I secretly collected a large amount of gold and precious stones, placed my affairs in God's hands and departed for Bokhara immediately. After prolonged investigations I found my brothers, took them to my house, enabled them to take a bath and gave them decent clothing. I refrained from talking about their conduct so as not to shame them. Instead, I bought goods to the value of one hundred and fifty toman for each and prepared for our departure; then we left for home. When we were within about two days' travelling distance from our city, I left my brothers in a village and returned to the city by myself. A few days later I made it known that my brothers were on their way back and that I would set forth on a certain day to receive them and to accompany them into the city.

Before dawn had broken, a weeping peasant came running to my house and knocked on the door, cursing and swearing. I asked him what had happened and he replied: "I only wish that the evil fate had never brought your brothers into our village!"—"But what has happened?" I asked. "A gang of robbers, their greed aroused by the sight of your brothers' wealth, has attacked our village and has robbed not only your brothers but has also plundered our poor huts."—"Where are my brothers now?"—"They are sitting in a corner of the city, naked and crying." I hurriedly brought them a few pieces of clothing and took them into my house. When our friends and acquaintances heard that my brothers had returned, they hurried to my house to welcome them. For twenty days I was kept busy looking after the guests so that I had hardly a moment's peace. When all this was over, I found that my brothers were even more ashamed than before. They spent their whole time in a corner of my house without having the slightest desire to go out. After this state of affairs had continued for three months, I considered it right to try and cheer them up a little and to undertake a journey together with them. Therefore, I discussed this with them one evening and said: "I feel like going on a journey with you and living in another country for a time. What do you think about the idea?"—"Brother," they said, "your plan is good and we have nothing against it."

When I saw that they agreed to my suggestion, I started to make preparations and bought goods suitable for selling in India. Then we made our way to a port. Soon our luggage and goods were on board, the sails were hoisted and we were rocking on the sea. Suddenly I noticed my dog running up and down along the beach in distress, making terrible noises. Finally he flung himself into the water but, try as he might, the waves kept driving him back to the beach until he was finally brought on board in a dinghy. He immediately jumped up to me, wagged his tail, gave all the signs of joy and then lay down quietly.

The ship continued on its path peacefully for a whole month. Without paying any attention to Satan's designs, I rejoiced repeatedly in seeing my brothers content; but

> Though you might be thinking only of peace,
> Satan will nevertheless hatch evil schemes.

My eldest brother had fallen in love with my slave girl and together with my other brother he secretly plotted against me. "How would you feel, brother," he said, "about getting rid of him? Then we should really be doing well. If we don't, our feeling of guilt towards him will finally be the end of us." And after they had discussed the idea at great length, they decided to throw me into the sea.

One night I lay in my cabin together with my slave girl. As dawn was breaking, my second eldest brother awoke me and said: "Do come out and see the strange things God has created." I staggered out, followed by my dog who had woken up at once. I saw my eldest brother standing at the railing, busily looking down at the waves. "What is going on, brothers?" I asked. "Come over here," they replied, "and see this strange group of sea creatures dancing under water, holding coral twigs in their hands." If anyone else but my brothers had told me such a story

I would not have believed them. However, I trusted their words. Heavy with sleep and still unsteady on my feet, I looked down—but no matter how I strained my eyes, I was unable to detect anything. "Can you not see anything?" my eldest brother asked me. At that instant my other brother came up from behind and pushed me into the water. The ship disappeared before my eyes like a shooting star. The waves tossed me continuously from one side to the other. One moment I was in a deep trough, the next high up on a crest. The waves struck me like whips so that I was near to surrendering my soul. My arms and legs refused to function and from the depths of my heart I addressed my lament to the throne of the only God. I begged him to save my life by the infinite treasure of his grace. Suddenly, as I was lying in the water, thrashing about with my arms and legs, I noticed something swimming towards me and then holding me above the surface whenever I threatened to drown. I opened my eyes and saw that it was my dog. When my brothers had thrown me overboard, he had jumped into the water at once and the Almighty God sent him to my rescue.

Supported by my faithful dog, I drifted about for seven days and nights on the dreadful sea until, in my helpless state, I was washed up on to a beach. Finally I struggled ashore on an island and fell down unconscious. When dawn broke I was awakened by my dog's barking. I thanked God for my rescue. Exhausted by drifting on the sea for such a long time, I was too weak to walk. When I looked around in all directions, I noticed a city in the far distance. Hoping to be able to obtain some food to keep me alive, I limped away towards the city. I fell down on the ground and rose up again. In this manner I continued until I reached the vicinity of the city by evening.

However, I was unable to move any farther and had to spend the night outside the wall, tortured by fatigue and hunger. It was not until the next morning that I entered the town.

When I reached the bazaar and saw the loaves of bread in the bakers' shops I nearly went out of my mind and my heart started beating wildly. I leant against a wall. I had no money to buy bread and I could not bring myself to beg for some. I sighed deeply and looked about sadly, but my pride prevented me from begging and I tried to comfort myself with the thought that I could beg for bread from another baker somewhere else, and so I passed several shops without finding the courage to beg. Finally, however, the hunger in my body became so fierce that it sapped my power of resistance and I felt as if the bird of my soul, in its greed for the life-giving grain, was about to burst the cage of my body with its mighty wings.

At that very moment two men appeared, dressed in Persian clothes. "God be praised," I said to myself, "for having saved me from the disgrace of begging from strangers! Who knows, maybe these men are acquaintances who would recognize me and give me something to eat without my having to ask for it." As they approached close enough for me to see their faces, I recognized them as my brothers and mortal enemies, but at that time I did not know yet what evil there was in their hearts.[8] Glad to see them well and happy, I hurried towards them, greeted them, threw myself down before their feet and kissed the ground.

At first they were transfixed with amazement at seeing me. The next moment, however, they uttered a loud cry, my second eldest brother kicked me brutally in the face and they both started attacking me with sticks. Beg as I might and ask for God's aid, it was of no avail; they continued to beat me and said: "What do you want from us, you cruel fiend?" People came running from all directions and asked what wickedness I had committed. My brothers tore the collars of their coats and burst out in loud laments: "This miserable wretch was our brother's servant. We were on a sea voyage and he threw our brother into the sea so that he drowned while he himself usurped our brother's immense wealth. We have searched for him for a long time in all the towns of India until we found him here today." Then they continued beating me and shouted: "You cruel, merciless and ungrateful lout! How could you find it in your heart to murder our young brother? What had he done to you?"

In the meantime, a few servants of the city governor had come along and heard these words. They arrested me and brought me before the governor, to whom they explained the whole matter. My brothers, who had followed us, lamented and cried for justice. They had bribed the governor with one hundred toman so that he would sentence me to death. The governor asked me about the accusation but the succession of terrible misfortunes that had befallen me, the suffering in the sea, the torture of hunger, the ill-treatment at the hands of my brothers and their wicked and despicable frauds, had completely robbed me of the power of speech so that I stood there, with my head bowed, unable to reply. The governor considered my silence as an admission of guilt and ordered me to be taken outside the city and hung from a gallows as a warning to others.

This is how my brothers, in return for my having released them some time ago from the stranglehold of the Jew for the sake of one hundred toman, had now sacrificed the same amount of money to put the noose around my neck. There I stood under the gallows and wherever I looked I saw no friend except God and this unfortunate dog which, while I was being taken to the gallows, threw himself before the feet of the people and rolled in the dust as if to beg them to release me. And although he was chased away with sticks, stones and kicks, he did not give up his attempts to touch the henchmen's hearts. When I saw myself deserted in this manner by all relatives and strangers, I exclaimed: "O God, come to my aid! There is no one besides you who could grant me refuge!" Then I pronounced my articles of faith and lost consciousness.

But God in his wisdom and justice arranged for the king of this city to be afflicted by a fierce attack of colic. All the physicians' efforts proved to be in vain and they were unable to ease his pains, which grew steadily worse. The Emirs and dignitaries of the realm were terrified and one of the viziers said: "There can be no safer means of restoring the king's health than to distribute gifts and to release the prisoners; the prisoners' blessings will then bring about the king's recovery." And so, one of the king's trusted men mounted his horse to arrange for the prisoners to be released as quickly as possible. When he came to the gallows, he spurred his horse, dispersed the crowd and cut my ropes so that I fell to the ground.

However, when my brothers saw how the situation was developing, they were afraid that if my life was spared I would pursue them, take my revenge and bring misfortune upon their heads. They therefore went to the governor and advised him to have my sentence carried out after all. The governor, who wanted to be helpful because of the money he had received from them, said: "At the moment it is impossible to have him executed publicly but to satisfy you, we shall have him thrown into Solomon's prison so that he can die of hunger and thirst without anybody ever learning what has happened to him. It is utterly impossible for him to escape from there." So the governor sent a few men to the public square to fetch me and to throw me secretly into Solomon's prison. This was a hole which the devils had dug at the top of a mountain peak on the orders of King Solomon. The prison was longer than the day is for pining lovers and darker than the night of separation, and all the criminals and wrong-doers who had incurred the king's wrath were thrown into that jail. I was thus taken to this hole of a prison and my brothers departed, their hearts relieved at having finally got rid of me.

Around midnight I regained consciousness and found myself in a very dark place filled by a revolting stench. I asked myself where I might have come to and when I remembered hanging at the gallows, I thought I must be in my grave and pronounced a few sacred words. Suddenly I heard the voices of two men. I was startled and commended my soul into God's protection. Then I observed a rope being lowered into the hole. Shortly afterwards I heard what sounded like people eating. This only increased my amazement. With my hands I tapped around in all directions but all I touched were decaying human skeletons. In my despair I cried out: "Oh, you creatures of God, where am I?" On hearing my words the two men burst into laughter and said: "You are in Solomon's prison and we are prisoners here."—"What are you eating?" I continued my questions: "Give me some of it." This brought about renewed laughter and when I repeated my request with greater urgency, they only spoke to me harshly. After they had eaten and drunk they lay down to sleep whereas I sat sleepless and crying, quite sapped of strength. For seven days and nights I had been tossed hither and thither by the waves until I had nearly given up all hope of rescue. When I had finally reached land and had been snatched from death at sea, had dragged myself into a city, hungry and thirsty, with bare feet and almost dying of hunger, I was beaten and ill-treated by my envious brothers and taken to the gallows, only to find myself finally in a deep dungeon.

When I was cast into the hole of a prison, my faithful dog lay down at the entrance. At midnight he saw a person tying a small parcel of bread and a jug of water to a rope, which was lowered into the hole, and a short while later the empty rope was pulled up again. It was evidently God's wish that the dumb animal should understand the idea that if someone was bringing bread and water to the people down there in the prison, he too must try and obtain bread and water for his master. As soon as dawn broke, the dog ran into the town. He slipped in through the city gate, went to a baker's shop and took up position nearby. After the baker had laid out the first loaves of bread and turned round to take the next batch from the oven, the dog jumped up, grabbed the bread and ran away. The baker chased after him, but although pursued with stones and sticks, the dog did not release the bread and ran to the dungeon as fast as he could. On the way he had to fight off hundreds of other dogs, but he managed to hold on to the bread until he reached the entrance. Then he dropped the bread, put his head through the opening and barked.

It was just one hour after sunrise when I heard something drop beside me and at the same time my dog's barks reached my ears. I greedily grabbed the bread and on looking up, I saw the opening of the dungeon above me like a shining star and realized that a new day had broken. I thanked God that the other two prisoners had not yet woken up. However, as soon as I had taken one bite of the bread I was overcome by such a thirst that I was unable to eat any more. In the meantime, the faithful animal, having provided me with bread, went away in search of water. At the foot of the mountain the dog noticed a village to which he ran. At the edge of the village an old woman had just filled her jugs with water and stood them in a cool place while she sat and spun. The dog ran into the courtyard towards the jugs. Just as the old woman approached to chase him away, he picked up a jug and ran away with it—but dropped it. He then tried the same with a second and third one and in that manner several jugs were broken and the water was spilled. The old woman grew cross and reached for a stick, but although she beat him, the dog stopped and looked at her so imploringly that finally she felt pity for him and placed before him one of the broken jugs which still contained some water. The dog, however, did not touch the water but rubbed his head against the woman's leg and gripped the seam of her dress with his teeth, as if trying to pull her out of the house and up the mountain. The woman thought that the animal wanted water for its puppies, and she took a jug full of water and went up the mountain with it. The dog showed her the way and now and again he would come up to her and rub against her leg. When she had finally reached the hole on the mountain top and the dog held on to her clothes and pulled the woman towards the hole, she realized that someone must be down there for whom the dog wanted water. She left the jug and went back to fetch a rope, the dog always at her heels. She returned with a rope, tied the jug to it and lowered it into the hole. At the same time the dog barked to attract my attention. Joyfully I took hold of the jug, released the rope and took a deep gulp of water which finally quenched my burning thirst. Then I ate heartily of the bread and afterwards lay down to sleep.

In this manner the kind animal supplied me with bread every morning, and later also brought me some water with the aid of the frail old woman. For a few days the baker had tried to prevent the dog from stealing bread but when the animal nevertheless continued to obtain bread by some means or other, the baker relented and preferred to throw it a loaf. When the dog found that the old woman was not yet on her way nor at the mouth of the dungeon, he ran down to her house and threw all the jugs about until the old woman, hoping for reward in paradise, became used to carrying water to the dungeon every morning. And after the dog had by his efforts provided me, the helpless prisoner, with bread and water, he probably found a piece of dry bread somewhere for himself, or a bone to chew; but for the remainder of the time he lay at the entrance to the dungeon.

I spent a full six months in this place. I thanked God for my rescue, but your majesty can imagine the condition a man must be in after having lived for six months at the bottom of a well where for him day was like the darkest night. I was weak and thin and alive only with half my soul; my body consisted only of skin and bones. Thus I lay one night, nearly blinded by the tears of suffering, and I sent this cry of lament to God's throne, bewailing my terrible fate to the heavens:

My cries arise to you from hollow cheeks, begging for freedom:
Let the light of day be cast upon the darkness of my path.

After I had thus spent two-thirds of the night in tears, God's mercy suddenly opened the gates of freedom for me. A rope was lowered into the depths and I heard a gentle voice say: "Unfortunate prisoner, take hold of the rope and tie it round your body. Your hour of liberation from this dungeon of suffering has come." I held on to the rope. After I had emerged from the dungeon, the darkness of the night prevented me from recognizing the man who had pulled me up. He was equally unable to see who I was but did not ask any questions. Instead, he started walking as soon as we had untied the rope from my body and said: "Now we must hurry, we cannot stay here." I crawled down the mountain on hands and knees until we reached a place where two saddled horses were waiting. The stranger told me to mount one, while he himself took the other, but apart from that observed complete silence. In this manner we rode out of the town and continued until we reached the sea-shore at dawn.

In the light of day I saw that my companion was a young man, well armed and of the most perfect beauty from head to toe. He suddenly stopped his horse. When I came quite close to him and his glance fell upon me, he turned towards me abruptly, bit his hand with anger, drew his sword and began attacking me. In mortal fright I threw myself on the ground, pronouncing the following words:

"Your generosity is now turning into cruelty,
Why has your friendship turned to wrath so suddenly?"

"You evil creature!" he exclaimed. "Who are you? How did you come to cross my path?" I replied: "Oh, stranger who has rescued me from death and snatched me from mortal peril, I am a foreigner, separated from all joy, who knows only misery and disappointment." My lament brought tears into the young man's eyes and softened his heart. He stopped attacking me and said: "Ride on, unfortunate man; this is not the place for conversation." He spurred his horse and without paying any further attention to me, he sighed and lamented and sang the following words:

"Oh, all hope in my heart is broken,
But everything happens in accordance with God's will."

And so he continued riding until we reached a resting place. There he dismounted and told me to get off my horse, too. He took off the saddle-bag and allowed the horses to graze, then he removed his weapons and sat down in the grass.

"Unfortunate one," he said to me, "tell me your story so that I may know who you are and what are the reasons for your suffering." And then I told him truthfully about my brothers' wickedness, without adding or leaving out anything. After he had listened to my sad story from the beginning to the end, tears flowed from his eyes and he said: "And now listen to what I have to tell you.

The Princess's Story

I AM the daughter of the great Radja who is the ruler of this land of Zairbad. The young man who was kept in Solomon's prison is called Behruz. He is the son of the minister at my father's court. One day the king ordered the sons of the Emirs to gather in the open square in front of the palace to compete with each other in knightly combat. At the same time he allowed the women of the harem to sit on the flat roof of the palace to watch the competition. We, the women, therefore took our places behind a many-coloured curtain woven with gold and from there we observed the games in a happy frame of mind. Then fate began to play its evil game with me and misfortune filled my cup to the brim. As it happened, Behruz defeated all the other Emirs' sons that day; besides, he was so beautiful and stately that my heart was filled with love for him. For a time I played secretly on the chess-board of romance while I was being carried on the wings of tenderness and smitten by the swords of love. Then I revealed to my old and faithful nurse the secret of my heart and gave her presents and beautiful clothes so that she would help me. She did indeed find ways and means of conducting the young man into my innermost and private chambers and I achieved the aim of my wishes. On beholding my beauty he also fell deeply in love. However, some time after we had become so well acquainted, a palace guard arrested the young man, who was dressed and armed like a warrior, outside the harem. The incident was immediately reported to the king and although he did not know what had driven the young man to such folly, he ordered him and his father to be executed. In response to urgent pleas from his courtiers he relented and had the two men thrown into prison instead.

Seven years have passed since then. I was so grateful that my lover's life had been spared and that nobody knew anything about my true feelings or had the faintest idea why he was found outside the harem, that I undertook personally to bring bread and water to the two prisoners without the people in the palace noticing anything. During all those years I went out there once a week with sustenance for seven days.

Last night, whilst thinking about the young man, I fell asleep. An angel appeared in my dream and said to me: 'Arise, prepare horses, make ready a saddle-bag with food and go up to that mountain, because tonight you will free your lover from prison.'

I jumped up joyfully and resolved to act boldly. I prepared everything as commanded by the voice and also took along a small box filled with precious stones. There can be no doubt that this vision came from the world beyond, and yet I was forced to discover that my beloved's guardian angel was asleep while yours watched over you. So be it, because it was decreed by fate!"

After she had spoken, she took some bread and a fried chicken from the saddle-bag. She poured brandy and rose-water into a beaker from a silver bottle and added sugar. She gave me a few pieces of bread and chicken and poured me a drink and also fed the dog, which had followed us. Then she took me to the edge of a brook and washed my face and body, cut my hair and nails and put clean clothes on me. Thereupon I turned my face towards Mecca and prayed. The lovely creature was highly surprised and asked me what I was doing. I replied: "I am praying to God to whom we owe reverence, the creator who is incomparable in his power, who has from his own strength created all beings simply by pronouncing the word of creation, the benevolent and merciful God who from the depth of his kindness has sent an angel like you to help me so that you may remove from the mirror of my suffering soul all the stains of misery and grief."

Briefly, I told her so much about God's miracles that I succeeded in banishing disbelief from the heart of the beautiful girl and she was intoxicated by the wine of my faith.

After a journey lasting two months we reached a city lying between the land of the Franks[10] and Zairbad. It was densely populated, even richer than Cairo and its climate was more pleasant than that of Kashmir. The king was a just ruler who cared for the well-being of his subjects. That is where we decided to stop. We equipped a suitable house for ourselves and purchased all the necessities. It so happened that in this town there lived a few Persians. They enjoyed greater esteem than most of the other inhabitants of the city and were on familiar terms with the dignitaries and noblemen. I joined them and after having recovered from the exertions of the journey, I made all the preparations for the marriage to my beautiful companion and then took her home as my legally wedded wife. After we had thus become united and I had become the lawful owner of the box containing the precious stones my noble wife had brought with her, I opened a jeweller's shop. Within three months I had already gained a considerable reputation and had made contact with the great and noble masters; I had made myself indispensable to my collaborators and the other merchants and had gained the most senior position among them. My fortunes improved from day to day, and the star of my luck had soon reached the zenith of its orbit.

One day, as I was walking through the streets of the city, on my way to visiting one of the great Emirs, I witnessed a crowd that had gathered in the open square. I went up and asked what was going on. "There are two Persians here," a man told me, "who are to suffer their punishment for robbery and murder." When I heard that, my own earlier experiences ran through my mind. I felt depressed and thought: "Who can be in a less fortunate position than he who is far away from his homeland and among strangers?" I hurriedly joined the crowd with an uneasy heart and suddenly I saw that the men concerned were my brothers. Bare-headed and bare-foot, wounded and with their hands tied to their backs, they were dragged across the ground to their place of punishment. Upon beholding this sight, my grieving heart filled with sorrow and bitter tears ran down my cheeks. I took the governor's servants to one side, gave them a handful of money and begged them to delay the execution for a short time. I then ran to the governor's house as fast as my feet would carry me and begged for mercy. I handed him a huge ruby which I had bought for five hundred toman. Kneeling in the dust before him, I humbly begged him to grant my request. The governor said: "Several people have accused the two men, convinced that the blood of innocent people is on their conscience, and the king has ordered that they are to suffer their punishment. There is but one way of rescuing them: the accusers have to be persuaded with gold to withdraw their accusation."

Following the governor's advice, I visited the plaintiffs and gave them five hundred toman. After having thus purchased my brothers' lives, I sent them to the baths and made them welcome in my house. This time, however, I hid my wife so that Satan would not again use my brothers for his evil schemes. I did, however, allow them to stay in my house; I helped them in every possible way and paid for their keep. I withdrew only during the night to sleep in the harem. Life went on for about a year in this manner. It so happened one summer's day that my full moon visited the baths. When entering the house on her return, she removed the veil from her face, unaware that two men were in the house. My second eldest brother saw her slim figure and her ravishing beauty and fell in love with her. After suffering the gnawing pain of longing for a while, he decided to kill me and secretly laid plans with my eldest brother. And while they made preparations to kill me, I was thanking God that my brothers had renounced their wicked way of life.

One evening, when we were sitting together talking, my eldest brother steered the conversation round to our homeland. The other sighed deeply. Another evening he talked about nothing except beautiful Persia, with the result that my eldest brother started crying and lamenting. Not dreaming what their true intentions were, I said to them: "Oh brothers, apples of my eyes! If you are thinking of our fatherland with such pain in your hearts, I would like you to know that I, too, long to return there. Be of good cheer because if it is God's will, we shall soon start our journey there." Later, when I was alone with my wife, I told her what had happened. She said: "I will gladly obey and do anything you consider right."

To cheer my brothers up, I hurriedly completed all the preparations necessary for the journey and my tents were erected in the plain. Many merchants and other travellers gathered in my camp. They regarded me as the leader of the caravan. At an hour when our stars were favourable, we started our journey with joy in our hearts. While we were travelling I hardly left my brothers for a minute and when I saw that their spirits were darkened by the dust of sorrow, I did my best to cheer them up.

After we had been travelling for one month, we had just set up our quarters one night and were sitting together talking, when one of my brothers said: "If we could arrange to have a day's rest here we could make a wonderful excursion tomorrow."—"What kind of excursion?" I asked. He replied: "We have been here before and spent a few days at this place. A short distance to the right there is a meadow. Through it flows a brook and the meadow is full of roses and tulips. It is only about one mile away from here. A river lovely as Salsabil[11] flows there and at its banks is the meadow whose scent of roses and hyacinths and other pleasant flowers is like the aroma of paradise." —"If this is so," I said, "we shall stay here tomorrow." The caravan was thus asked to stop for a day. I gave orders for our breakfast to be prepared very early next morning. My brothers arose before daybreak and prepared for the excursion. They came to wake me and to please them I dressed immediately and ordered my horse to be brought. "No," they said, "if we ride we would miss half the pleasure of this beautiful countryside. It is much better to walk." We then took a few slaves, narghiles and coffee with us and set forth. We also took bows and arrows and as soon as the sun had risen, we began to shoot for pleasure. This dog, which has always brought me good luck, followed me as usual, sometimes running in front and sometimes behind us.

After we had walked some distance, my brothers sent one slave back to the caravan under some pretext. We continued for some time and then they found another pretext for sending the second slave after the first. Meanwhile, they kept talking to distract my attention. We walked on and on but found neither a green meadow nor a spring. After having walked for a further mile, I had to follow the call of nature. I therefore put my bow down and looked for a lonely spot. It was then that my brothers tried to murder me. They had concealed their swords under their cloaks and when they thought a good opportunity had presented itself, they drew their swords and rushed at me. My eldest brother swung his weapon and hit me with such force that he nearly split my head in two. All I was able to utter was: "Murderer! What are you doing?", and then the other dealt me such a severe blow that I fell to the ground and thought that death was near. These two cruel stony-hearts, however, continued to beat me with their swords; I felt the blows everywhere, in my back and loins, on my arms and legs and on my head. The unfortunate dog attacked them, bit them and tore their clothes with his teeth until they dealt him a few blows as well so that he fell down unconscious. Then these two wolves in human disguise inflicted a few wounds on themselves and hurried away as if driven by fear, returned to the caravan and raised the alarm: "Escape, friends, and hurry away as quickly as you can so that you may save your lives and your belongings from destruction! We have been attacked by a gang of robbers who inflicted these wounds on us, and now they are after us."

As soon as the people in the caravan heard the word robber, they took fright and moved off as quickly as they could. My royal pearl, with whom I was united by the bond of marriage, knowing of my brothers' earlier misdeeds, killed herself with a dagger.

The desolate plain in which my brothers had abandoned me belongs to the land of the Franks, and one of their cities was not far away. In that city stood a large temple belonging to the Franks and all the kings of those provinces therefore owed allegiance and paid their taxes to the city. The king of this city had a daughter who was beautiful and glorious beyond measure; her beautiful face and her black ringlets enchanted kings and princes. Since the women are not kept away from the men in that part of the world, the princess, together with other beautiful women, took part every day in hunts and excursions into the countryside. It so happened that the king had a garden in the plain, and during these very days the princess had left the city to stay in that place with her father's permission, in order to spend a month or so walking and hunting. She had therefore taken up residence in the garden.

The same day this world-illuminating sun was on a hunting excursion and came riding along with her servants and confidants. They were all intoxicated and in a happy mood. They had split up into several smaller groups for fun, and rode out in different directions. It so happened that the princess, together with a number of beautiful girls, came to the spot where I lay unconscious. My dog's cries had brought her to the place, and when she saw my desperate condition she immediately jumped down from her horse and sat down by my side. She sent a messenger to her surgeon, who was always close by, and said to him: "Try to snatch this ill-treated servant of our great God from the arms of death and make him well again with your medicines; then you can be sure of a coat of honour and gifts and other favours." The skilful physician agreed to make the attempt. On the orders of the most beautiful princess, I was laid on a carpet and carried into the garden. The helpless dumb animal dragged itself behind us and also entered the garden with me. Here, the clever Frankish doctor began his treatment as instructed by the beautiful woman. He cleansed my body of dust and blood, stitched up the wounds and covered them with plasters. Instead of ordinary water he poured rose-water, in accordance with the Frankish custom, down my throat and made sure that I was nursed most carefully. The royal pearl visited me twice or three times a day at my sick-bed, fed me personally with sorbet and said in a lamenting voice: "Who might be the cruel ruffian who has treated a servant of the great Lord in such a foul manner, and is not afraid of God's vengeance and retribution?"

This princess with the sugar-sweet lips came every night to visit me after the servants had gone to bed. She approached my sad sick-bed entirely on her own, sat down beside me, gave me wine and brandy to drink and showed me kindness and mercy beyond description. After one month had passed, my wounds had healed and the beautiful princess then kept her promise to the surgeon and gave him a coat of honour and other presents, because she was delighted beyond measure about my health having been restored. The thorn of love had pierced her bosom and the seed of tenderness germinated in her heart.[12]

To be brief, we became lovers and she decided to escape with me. As a few merchants from Iran, Turkestan and Khorasan were about to sail from one of the country's ports, I joined them and embarked with the princess, who was disguised as a slave girl, and the dog. However, before we had left the harbour, the ship was stopped and searched by the governor of the port. The king had discovered his daughter's flight and in order to have her returned without revealing her shameful deed, he had given orders at once to all the princes and those who were in charge of border posts and ports, not to let any traveller pass without investigating whether he had any slave girls with him. Any slaves they found were to be sent to his residence so that he could select those he liked best. The merchants on board our ship who had beautiful slave girls with them, hid them in their crates and I, too, hid the princess in the same manner—but the governor nevertheless found all the women and took them away with him. In the evening they were all returned, with the exception of the princess, and the merchants were given permission to sail. I, however, left the ship in despair and spent all my time searching for my beloved.

First I went to the king's residence, but my enquiries there only proved to me that the princess had not returned to her father. Then I went back to the port, since I assumed that the governor had kept her for himself. Finally I succeeded in secretly entering the governor's harem, where I did find my beloved and was able to conduct a secret conversation with her. On her advice I, as a wronged person, sought solace in the temple of the Gods of the Franks, complaining that a mighty man had robbed me of my wife. An old, venerable and holy woman who was the most powerful of all the priests and who was called "Mother of the Brahmins" took up my case; her influence and power were so great that she forced the king to give me satisfaction. The king appointed me governor of the city and left it to me to take revenge on the previous governor, and to regain my alleged wife, because the king was unaware that it was his own daughter who had disappeared. I personally killed the governor, released my beloved from his harem and married her. The king was most gracious to me and appointed me one of his advisers.

Three years later a caravan of merchants arrived in this port. Nearly all of them came from Zairbad and wanted to reach Persia by sea. It was customary for a caravan entering this city to bring me presents through their leaders and to invite me to a banquet the following day. On such occasions I would examine their goods and receive the tithe, following which they would be granted permission to continue their journey. By virtue of this ancient custom, the people in this particular caravan also came to see me, presented their compliments and invited me to their banquet. When I examined their goods the following day, I discovered my two brothers who were in the service of the leader of the caravan. They came along, carrying bales of goods on their shoulders and under their arms. Their loads were so heavy that no servant should have been expected to carry them. Enraged by this sight I said to myself: "It is inhuman for you to live in happiness and plenty while your brothers have to spend their life in such abject misery." When I returned home I took them with me. I showed them all possible kindness, found them a suitable occupation and tried my best to help them to gain honour and respect.

These two incorrigible men, however, were unable to appreciate their good fortune. Once again they hatched new schemes to murder me. One night, when everyone was asleep, they approached my bed with swords in their hands, and it was again this faithful and clever dog who attacked them first. Only then the guards came rushing in and arrested them.

Your majesty, by now my patience had come to an end. However, I could not bring myself to condemn them to death and so I decided to lock them up; for that reason I had them put into these cages so that I could always keep a watchful eye on them and need not fear that they would again do something evil. This is the reason for the wretched state in which you see them and why I treat the dog with such honour.

Many years passed, the princess bore me several children who, alas, died at an early age and even the princess herself was soon called away to God's mercy. As a result of those losses my life of wealth became repugnant to me and I began to find the land of the Franks insufferable. I begged the king to let me go, took my two brothers and the dog along and travelled to Persia. In order that nobody should learn about the crimes committed by my brothers, I suffered the disgrace of being regarded as a dog worshipper and for that reason I had to pay a special tax in Persia for a long time. But now this young man has brought me here and I have been shown the great honour of being allowed to appear before the king—and this is the end of my story.'

When I had heard this report, I turned to the supposed merchant's son and asked him: 'Are you a son of the people of this land?' He kissed the ground and asked my forgiveness, continuing: 'Your majesty, may your fortune flower for ever. What I, your humble subject, have done was for my father's sake. I am the daughter of your vizier whom your majesty had imprisoned, although he is an old man and not guilty of any crime. I am his only child, and this is why I felt obliged to do everything possible for his liberation. I therefore travelled to Persia without the knowledge of my relatives and friends. From there I brought with me this man so that your majesty may behold him with your own eyes, and the illustrious men gathered here can see that my father had spoken the truth.'

When it was thus revealed that the supposed young man was the daughter of the vizier, the merchant uttered a sorrowful sigh and fell to the ground unconscious. He came to soon afterwards and said: 'Woe betide me! All my efforts have been in vain. At my age I have accepted the hardships of the journey and have torn the veil from my secret, without obtaining the goal of my wishes!'—'What were your wishes?' I asked. He replied: 'As I have no longer any children, I wanted to accept this companion of mine in place of my son, but this hope, too, has been shattered by the tricks of cruel fate.'

My heart bled with pity for this severely tested man; I called him nearer and promised him this beautiful girl as his wife. This calmed him immediately. Then I arranged for the young girl to be taken to the harem. To her father, however, I sent a horse and a coat of honour, had him taken from the prison into the baths and then had him brought to the court with full honours. I went out to meet him in person, pressed him to my heart as if he were my own father, kissed his forehead and allowed him to take his seat again on the high chair of the viziers. As far as the merchant was concerned, I gave him a coat of honour and appointed him to a high office and then I ordered the whole city to be decorated for the festivities, and in a blessed hour I had the marriage celebrated between the vizier's daughter and the merchant. And from then onwards the merchant lived for many years happily by the side of his young wife.

19. THE GAZELLE AND THE MOUSE

A HUNTSMAN had spread his net in the wide open plain. A gazelle happened to pass, and as misfortune would have it, it was trapped in the net. The other gazelles, who had witnessed this sad event, left it to its fate.

Meanwhile a mouse came out of its hole. The unfortunate gazelle asked the mouse for help and begged for assistance in escaping, but the mouse replied: 'It would be the height of folly to place one's head in a noose voluntarily. Therefore, if I were anxious to undo the knots of your net, I might easily break my teeth trying to do so and I would suffer only trouble and hardship. The huntsman is approaching, and if I helped you escape from your prison and your peril, and became trapped myself, the huntsman in his wrath would destroy my home and wreak ruin and disaster upon me. You are neither friend nor foe to me.' The gazelle replied: 'It's true you don't know me or call me your friend, but generosity at least should make you set me free.' The mouse, however, objected: 'If your freedom didn't mean a thousand dangers for me, if your good fortune would not mean disaster for me, I wouldn't hesitate to do as you wish.'—'But,' said the gazelle, 'those who are of noble birth and aristocratic blood consider it normal to suffer for the benefit of others.

> He whose noble deeds are remembered
> Will always be well spoken of.

Ancient wisdom teaches us that he who could free a

living being from harm and suffering, and who could help those that have lost their way to reach their destination, should not stand there shamefacedly: he shall be spared the sufferings of hell.'

The mouse, however, paid no attention to these words and was about to return to its hole when a hen-harrier seized it in its claws. At that moment the huntsman arrived. He saw how beautiful the gazelle was and said: 'I would rather sell it alive.' Just then a man happened to pass who was God-fearing and free of any falsehood, dressed in the garments of the devout, and his appearance bore the mark of humility. He asked the huntsman the price of the gazelle. 'The price is one piece of gold,' replied the huntsman. The devout servant of the Lord said: 'He who rescues an unfortunate creature from death will himself be spared destruction.' And so he bought the gazelle and allowed it to run free.

20. THE CAMEL RIDER AND THE SERPENT

ON his travels a camel rider reached a place where a few caravan travellers had lit a fire. After they had moved on, the wind fanned the flames and a big fire ensued. The sparks were flying in all directions over the steppe, and the dried shrubs started burning fiercely everywhere so that the desert resembled a field of tulips. In the midst of the flames lay a large serpent whose escape routes had all been cut off by the flames, so that it was unable to get away in any direction and was about to be roasted like a fish in the pan or a partridge on the spit. Blood started dripping from the serpent's eyes, which were swollen with venom, and when it saw the camel rider it asked him for help, saying:

'Will you not be merciful to me?
Do help me escape from my agony!'

The camel rider was a devout and kind man and when he heard the serpent's lament and saw its misery and helplessness, he thought: 'There is no doubt that the serpent is man's enemy, but now it is in extreme danger and in dire need of help. The best I can do, therefore, is to be merciful and to sow the seed of magnanimity in the soil of action, whose fruits can bear nothing but happiness in this world and bliss in the next.' With these thoughts he tied his game-bag to the tip of his spear and held it out. The serpent made use of the opportunity and slipped into the game-bag. The huntsman rescued it from the flames, believing that he had done a good deed. Then he opened the bag and said to the serpent: 'Now crawl away anywhere you like, and show your gratitude for having been rescued from this peril by withdrawing into the wilderness and not harming mankind in future, because he who commits acts of injustice will be cursed in this world and his foes will rejoice at his fate in the next.

Fear God and be good throughout the days of your life
So that you will not have to fear death.'

'Do stop your silly talk,' said the serpent, 'I will not leave here until I have bitten you and your camel.'—'What?' asked the rider. 'Have I not done you a good turn by rescuing you from the flames? Is that to be my reward—and do you really believe this would be fair and just?

I showed you friendship and responded to your pleas
Am I to be rewarded with bitter injustice?'

'Yes,' replied the serpent, 'although you have done a good deed for me, you were ill-advised to do so. You bestowed kindness on someone unworthy of it. You knew perfectly well that I am a harmful creature and that mankind cannot expect anything good from me. Well, you have gone to the trouble of rescuing me and have thereby done a good turn for someone you should have treated badly. Therefore, suffering is only a just reward for your action because showing kindness to evil is like ill-treating the good.

Reason and faith in their holy alliance
Do neither allow the good and noble to be hurt

Nor kindness to be shown to the evil ones
Whose minds are filled only with death and wickedness.'

The rider spoke again: 'Be fair and just. What religion would allow us to reward good with evil and what moral upholds the view that the purity of a good deed may be rewarded with the filth of an evil one?'—'It is customary among you humans,' replied the serpent, 'and now I shall act in accordance with your principles and sell you the goods I bought at your bazaar of justice.

Gain for an hour that which you sell throughout the year.'

All the objections the man raised were in vain. The serpent merely said: 'Decide quickly whether I should first bite you or your camel.'—'Abandon this absurd idea,' said the man, 'to reward good with evil can never bring happiness.' The serpent, however, was adamant: 'This is the custom among humans and I will follow their example.' The rider disputed the serpent's words and said: 'If you can prove to me and produce witnesses to testify that it is customary among humans to settle debts in this manner, I shall gladly surrender my life to you and seek death without offering any resistance.'

The serpent looked around and saw a buffalo cow grazing in the steppe. 'Come,' said the serpent, 'and let us discover the truth with the help of this buffalo cow.' The serpent and the camel rider approached the buffalo cow and the serpent spoke first: 'Tell me, what is the reward for a good deed?'—'If you want to know how humans behave in this respect,' replied the buffalo cow, 'I can tell you that good deeds are rewarded with evil. Listen to my story: for some time I had my home with a human being. Each year I presented him with a calf and I filled his larder with milk and butter and his entire household and livelihood depended on me. When I grew old and was unable to bear any more calves, he was no longer prepared to care for me and drove me from his house out into the steppe. After grazing here for some time without having to do any work I gradually gained weight. One day, my former master came out. He thought I had grown fat enough and so he called a butcher and sold me to him. Today they will come and take me to the slaughter-house to kill me. That is my reward for all the good deeds I performed for them.

That is my fate and who will listen to my plea?'

'There,' said the serpent to the rider, 'you heard for yourself. Now hurry and prepare yourself to receive my bite.'—The camel rider, however, raised objections. 'According to law, no judgment can be passed on the basis of one witness only. Find a second witness and then you may act as you see fit.'

The serpent looked around again and noticed a tree. 'Let us go and ask that tree over there,' said the serpent. The camel rider agreed. They went up to the tree and the serpent asked: 'What is the reward for a good deed?' The tree replied: 'According to a man's principles, good deeds are rewarded by evil ones and beneficial actions by harmful ones. I am able to offer proof of this: As you can see, I am a tree growing here in the steppe. I give comfort to all passers-by. If a traveller crossing this barren land comes along, plagued by heat and fatigue, he is only too glad to rest in my shade for a while to recuperate.

When he opens his eyes afterwards he thinks: "That branch up there would make an excellent handle for my axe, and the one over there would be ideal for my spade. The trunk would make a splendid board or a very good door." If he has an axe or a saw with him he will cut from my branches or trunk whatever he likes and in return for the rest I offered him he will only inflict pain upon me.

While I try to give him shade,
He unfeelingly takes my life in return.'

'There you are,' said the serpent to the camel rider, 'now you have heard two witnesses. It is now your turn to surrender your life and let me bite you.'—'Life is so precious,' said the man, 'and it is so hard to tear one's heart away from the good things in life as long as the tiniest spark of hope remains. If a third witness were to express the same views on this matter, I would sacrifice my life without further hesitation and submit to God's will.'

As fate would have it, a fox was standing nearby. He had observed everything and had listened to their conversation attentively. 'Very well,' said the serpent, 'let us ask the fox over there and hear what he has to say.' However, before the camel rider had time to ask the fox, he raised his voice and spoke: 'How is it you do not know that good is rewarded with evil? What kindness have you shown this serpent to deserve such punishment?' The man told the fox what had happened. The fox replied: 'You appear to be a sensible man. Why, then, do you tell all these lies?

I always think the wise man speaks the truth,
It ill becomes the mouth of the sage to tell lies.'

'He is telling the truth,' the serpent intervened; 'you can see the game-bag hanging from the saddle strap over there. This is what he used for rescuing me from the flames.' The fox, however, grew excited: 'Do not try to tell me that there is enough room in that small bag for such a large serpent!'—'If you refuse to believe it,' said the serpent, 'I am willing to crawl back into the bag so that you can see it with your own eyes.'—'Yes, if I could see it with my own eyes,' the fox replied, 'and verify the truth of your claim, I should be ready to pronounce a fair judgment on both of you, without deceit and free of self-interest.' The man opened the game-bag and the serpent, persuaded by the fox's words, crawled into it. Thereupon the fox said: 'Young man, if you have your enemy at your mercy, do not spare him.

If the foe has been placed into your hand,
Be wise and do not spare his life.'

The man followed this advice, closed the game-bag and kept striking it against the ground until the serpent was dead and the last spark of its malice was extinguished, so that all living creatures were safe from its evil intentions.

It is well to kill those who lead evil lives.
He who kills evil does a kindness to others.

21. THE OLD WOMAN AND HER DAUGHTER

A WOMAN, who had led a long life of poverty, had a daughter called Mahasti. The full moon envied the radiant beauty of her cheeks and the illustrious sun was hot with shame because of the reflection of her breathtaking face.

One sweet word from her and reason is silenced,
The confectioner must bow down before her in shame;
One smile—and death will race through the land,
One tender look—and the world is aflame.

Suddenly, malevolent fate struck the rosy-cheeked cypress. Her head sank back on the pillows of her sick-bed and yellow crocus flowered in the garden of her beauty instead of red roses. The freshness of her face, comparable to young jasmin, was driven out by a feverish glow and the abundant hyacinth ringlets lost their gloss in the fire of her illness.

Deprived of the fullness of young spring,
She grew thin as a musk hair.

The old woman never left her daughter's bedside, and with eyes damp as a spring cloud, she cried and wailed: 'Oh, sweet child who are your mother's life, if only I could sacrifice that life for you. Would that I, worn out and beaten down by misery and suffering, could be dust under your feet! How I wish I could sacrifice myself to make you well again. I would gladly surrender half of the life I am still dragging around with me, so that you may live! Every morning she uttered sighs and laments: 'Lord, be merciful to this young creature who has not yet seen anything of the world and take me, an old and ailing woman, tired of life, in her place.

Oh, take the days allotted to me
And add them to her span of life.
If suffering has made me into a shadow of my former self,
Do not touch a hair on her head!'

The old woman was so full of motherly love and feeling that she spent the day and night in devout prayer and deep lament and would have gladly bought her daughter's life with her own.

It so happened that one day a cow belonging to the old woman returned from the field and walked into the kitchen. Attracted by the smell of soup, it put its head into the pot and drank all the soup. However, when the cow wanted to withdraw its head from the pot, it was unable to do so. Angrily, it stormed about in the kitchen, with the pot stuck on its head. The old woman was out at the time and did not know what was going on. When she returned and saw a creature of such strange appearance running about in the house, she thought it was the angel of death who had come for Mahasti's soul. In her panic, the old woman cried:

'Prince of death! I am not Mahasti!
I am but a wretched old woman.
If you are looking for the girl's soul,
You will find her body in the chamber over there!
Take away Mahasti for whom you are looking,
And leave me here in peace.'

So we see, when man is threatened by peril,
His first thoughts are for himself.

Notes and Sources

For full comparisons of motifs and a history of Persian folk-literature, the reader is referred to the German edition, *Persische Marchen* (Diederichs, Düsseldorf, 1958).

1. *The Story of Ali Muhammad's Mother*

Source: manuscript collection of Mrs Munschîzâdeh.

(1) In the eastern part of Shiraz there is a mountain on the summit of which there is a deep ravine called Tcha Qala Bandar, also known as the Well of Death.

(2) Sakine and Gul Banu are girls' names.

(3) Rammals are fortune tellers who claim to be able to discover secret things with the aid of their Ramls, which usually consist of a board and a few dice or a dish filled with sand into which astrological signs can be scratched.

2. *The Bird called Flower Trill*

Source: manuscript collection of Mrs Munschîzâdeh.

(1) Gulabetum: a legendary country.

(2) Qaf mountains: a mountain range at the end of the world.

(3) This passage is superfluous within the overall framework of the story; the hairs are not used. An episode in which they are used has probably been omitted.

3. *Muhammad the Shepherd and the Peri Princesses*

Source: manuscript collection of Mrs Munschîzâdeh.

4. *The Black Foal*

Source: manuscript collection of Mrs Munschîzâdeh.

(1) Kallepazi: a man who boils sheep's and lambs' heads for food.

5. *The Bald Herdsman*

Source: *Tschähârdah äfsâneh* (Teheran 1906), ch. 4.

(1) This custom is still practised in the area of the mountains around Kerman.

(2) i.e. the full moon.

(3) i.e. a prostitute who deserves to have her hair cut off. This was one of the punishments meted out to women found guilty of being unchaste.

6. *The False Chief Rammal*

Source: *Tschähârdah äfsâneh* (Teheran 1906), ch. 12.

(1) Rammals are fortune tellers who claim to be able to discover secret things with the aid of their Ramls, which usually consist of a board and a few dice, or a bowl filled with sand into which astrological signs can be scratched.

(2) The dinar existed only as a unit of calculation and not as a coin. The toman is a gold coin, the qran a silver coin. One toman was equal to ten qran. One qran, which up to devaluation in the 1890s was equivalent to rather more than £1, was divided into twenty shahi or a thousand dinar. Ashrafi was the name of an old-fashioned thin gold coin.

(3) By the sword and the Koran which they carried with them.

(4) This is a literal expression, corresponding roughly to the saying: 'The pitcher goes so often to the well that it comes home broken at last.'

7. *The Secret of the Baths of Bad'gard*

Source: *Oisseje Hâtim Tâï* (Bombay 1899).

(1) Hatim of the tribe of Tai, who was one of the poets of the desert Arabs in the days before the prophet Mohammad, is revered in legends as an example of a noble bedouin chief. To help Prince Munir gain the hand of the beautiful Queen Husn Banu in marriage, Hatim undertook to answer seven questions on the prince's behalf. The solution of these problems was the

queen's condition imposed upon her suitors. The last of these seven tasks was the unveiling of the secret surrounding the baths of Bad'gard.

(2) During an earlier adventure.

(3) A clay vessel for wine or similiar drinks.

(4) The story is confused at this point. According to the original wording Hatim has correctly taken the road leading to the left, along which he continues. However, it would appear from the old counsellor's reproaches that Hatim is still on the road he was advised to avoid. The translation has been altered accordingly.

(5) According to an older legend, Gayomard was the first man, according to later versions, the first king on earth.

(6) 'Bad'gard' means 'Castle in the Air', i.e. an imaginary castle.

(7) The staff of a bath includes a barber whose duty is to shave the heads of male visitors. The mirror is part of his equipment.

(8) One Mitqal is said to be equivalent to 4.6 grammes.

8. *Muhammad the Master Marksman*

Source: manuscript collection of Mrs Munschîzâdeh.

(1) See 6, note 2.

9. *Sa'd and Sa'id*

Source: *Tschihil tûtî* (Teheran 1924), 16ff.

(1) The last few words are omitted from the text but have been added from the context. The storyteller forgot that originally he had talked about two chickens.

(2) Iram is a wonderful city often mentioned in Arabic legend, hidden in a far-away desert. It was given to only very few people to see that city by chance.

(3) In this last passage a few words have been added here and there to make the story, greatly abbreviated at this point, more easily comprehensible.

10. *The Three Comrades*

Source: D. C. Phillott, Some Current Persian Tales, Memoirs of the Asiatics Society of Bengal (Calcutta 1906), No. 2.

(1) The stranger was expected to appear before the Kadi as the woman's husband and declare that he wanted to be divorced from her, so that she could marry again after having been divorced according to law.

(2) A kind of sweet paste, prepared from sugar and flour.

11. *The Valuable Birds*

Source: Arthur Christensen: *Contes persanes en langue populaire* (Copenhagan 1918), No. 8.

12. *The Dog's Last Will*

Source: Christensen, op. cit., No. 18.

13. *The Deaf Man*

Source: Christensen, op. cit., No. 26.

14. *The Physician and his Son*

Source: Christensen, op. cit., No. 24.

15. *The Surety*

Source: Christensen, op. cit., No. 31.

16. *The Three Schoolmasters*

Source: Christensen, op. cit., No. 49.

(1) An Akhund is a man who has studied, especially theology: the term is frequently used in a derogatory sense for a pedantic person.

(2) It was customary at school for the children to clap their hands and to call 'Bless you!' whenever one of them had to sneeze.

(3) Friday is the Mohammedan weekly day of rest.

17. *The Land of Happiness*

Source: *'Inâjätu'llâh Kanbû. Bähâr-i-dânisch*, Lucknow 1896, pp. 309ff.

(1) Near Agra in India.

(2) The Persians frequently refer to sky as being green.

(3) A town in northern India.

(4) The constellation Pisces.

(5) Khizr was a prophet who had drunk from the spring of life, thus becoming immortal. He accompanied Alexander the Great on his search for the spring of life. He is a very old mythical figure in the Islamic version.

(6) Manes, the founder of the Manichaean religion, was according to legend a painter of unsurpassed skill.

(7) According to the ancient Persian calendar, Farvardin is the first month of the year. As the year begins with the vernal equinox, Farvardin is the actual month of spring. Incidentally, Persia has reintroduced the old names of the months in place of the Arabic ones, which were previously used in the official calendar.

(8) Kavzar is a river in paradise.

(9) 'Sorceress,' 'female conjurer.'

(10) Iram is a wonderful city often mentioned in the Arabic legend, hidden in one of the distant deserts. Only a very few people were privileged to see the city by chance.

(11) Rizvan is the name of the angel who guards the gate of paradise.

(12) Barbad was a famous musician who lived during the reign of the Sassanid King Khusrav II (590-628 A.D.).

(13) According to the Arabic fable, he was King Solomon's vizier.

(14) Khuzistan, the ancient Susiana, has a mild climate where sugar could be grown.

(15) The love of Madjnun ('the mad one') and Leila is one of the best-loved themes in Arabic and Persian poetry.

18. *The Dog with the Ruby Necklace*

Source: *Tschähâr Därwisch* (Lahore, n.d.), pp. 88ff.

(1) The Byzantine, later the Ottoman Empire.

(2) A country in Pamir on the upper reaches of the river Oxus (Amu Darjas), famous for its rubies and other precious stones.

(3) One Mithkal is stated to be equivalent to 4.6 grammes.

(4) A formula pronounced by Mohammedans in the face of threatening dangers and horrors.

(5) High priests, descendants of Mohammad.

(6) This presumably refers to the market square of the same name in Ispahan.

(7) The governor's henchmen are men who inflict corporal punishment on insolvent debtors. In accordance with Persian custom, they are beaten on the soles of their feet, which also follows from the context of the story.

(8) This last remark, indicating that the storyteller did not yet know that his brothers had deliberately thrown him overboard, is not found in the Persian text but is taken from the translation of the Hindustani version by L. F. Smith. Without such an addition the whole situation fails to make sense.

(9) A territory south-east of Bengal.

(10) This refers evidently to the European colonies in India.

(11) A river in paradise.

(12) The following section of the very involved story—up to the point where the storyteller is appointed governor—is presented here in a much condensed form.

19. *The Gazelle and the Mouse*

Source: Mohammed Ibn Ghazi de Malatya, *Le Jardin des Esprits* (tr. H. Massé) (Publications de la Société des études iraniennes 14, Paris 1938).

20. *The Camel Rider and the Serpent*

Source: Husain Wâ'iz al-Kâschifî, *Anvar-l-Sutailî* (Teheran,

1921), pp. 163ff.

21. *The Old Woman and her Daughter*
Source: As 18, pp. 284ff.